FEAVER PITCH

GRAHAM TEMPEST

BRIGHTWAY PRESS

Oliver Steele novels by Graham Tempest:

    CASINO CARIBBEAN

    CASINO EXCELSIOR

    CASINO QADDAFI

    CASINO DE FRANCE

    CASINO HAVANA

    JOBURG STEELE

    FEAVER PITCH

FEAVER PITCH
A Brightway book
bpi#210306

Brightway Press Inc.
522 Hunt Club Blvd, #316
Apopka, Florida 32703

ISBN (Print edition) 978-0-9996727-3-0

1

"**K**on? This Is Pedro. It's about Bruno. It's bad news."

I usually screen calls when I'm at home at my cabin on Coquina Key but Pedro is someone I like and trust, so when I heard his voice on the speaker I took this one.

I picked up the phone. "What?"

"He's been shot. He's dead, Kon."

It took me a moment to react. Bruno was the closest thing I had to a best friend. But death, alas, is something I am very familiar with. Years ago, I was a fighter pilot in the Israeli Air Force, although they fired me after a year for being drunk most of the time. I've had a bumpy career since then, first as a mercenary in Africa and then as a small-time drug dealer in Miami. But nowadays, despite ferrying refugees from Cuba to Florida which is what I do for a living, my life is mostly non-violent.

"What happened?"

"I don't know. I came round to take him to breakfast as we arranged last night when we met at a party on Star Island, and found his body."

"Have you called the police?"

"I'm about to."

"But you called me first?"

"Yes."

We both knew why. The three of us had history.

Last year I very nearly died in Cuba. In the course of a boat run I was arrested on a beach near Havana, taken to a prison island and locked in a cage for three days without food or much hope of surviving. Pedro and Bruno, along with my well-spoken English friend Oliver Steele, rescued me. Afterwards Bruno, not surprisingly, found it prudent to leave Cuba. He now lives – or lived – in Coral Gables, a decent but not grand suburb of Miami.

It was at least possible that Bruno's death had to do with enemies he made during that episode. Either way, Pedro and I would have strong opinions about what should be done to his killer.

"I'll come round," I said.

"How long?"

"About an hour. Must you call the police?"

"I think so, but not right away. They don't know what time I got here so they won't know how long I waited before phoning them." Pedro lives in Hialeah, ten miles north of Coral Gables, along with many other second and third generation Cuban Americans.

"I hear you."

I got into my '97 Jeep Grand Cherokee V8, bright red with gold trim. I started the engine, stopped and thought. I got out, went back into the house, fetched the Glock 19 from the kitchen drawer and shoved it in my pants pocket, then headed up the road.

With my foot down hard I made it to Coral Gables in forty minutes. I love the Jeep dearly, but it's an electricity hog and if I don't use it almost daily the battery goes flat, so it welcomed the mileage.

Bruno's apartment was on the second floor of a down-at-heel two storey building of a dozen units, a couple of blocks south of the glitzy Cuban diner Versailles. The downstairs entrance to the once-white structure boasted a lock but it was broken, so I pushed my way in and climbed uncarpeted concrete stairs. Without air conditioning the atmosphere was damp and muggy, typical Miami in August.

The flat was a small one-bedroom but at least it was cool. In the narrow hallway Pedro greeted me, looking grim. "In there." He pointed to the living room.

Bruno's slim body lay on its back on the floor. His pale torso wore black boxer shorts and a blood-stained towelling robe. He had been shot several times. Proximate cause of death was a through-and-through hole in the middle of his chest, barely a trickle of blood in front, but behind, a mess of blood and human tissue, spread in a pool on the worn carpet. Some of the blood had spattered an open newspaper, yesterday's Miami Herald, that lay partly underneath the body.

But it was the other wounds that shocked me. A bullet in each knee, neither of them fatal but both unimaginably painful, showing sadism by the killer. A choice had apparently been made not just to end the young man's life, but to inflict maximum suffering.

Probably to make a point, too – for the minutes or hours it took to snuff out his life. The shooter wanted Bruno not just to know his killer but to acknowledge, through a haze of agony, why he was being killed. For that, one knee would have been enough. As for the second knee, what sort of sadist would do that? What did he say to Bruno between the first and the second bullet? That he was going to double the punishment, ratchet up the pain? Such sadistic behaviour suggested the worst kind of human predator.

I looked at Pedro, who nodded. Hard to describe how I felt at that moment, but quiet fury about covers it.

I owed Bruno a lot. My arrest in Cuba occurred just as I was about to run a boatload of refugees back to the States. It's a service I still provide despite some political changes since then. Things have quietened down a bit in that department since the death of Fidel Castro. President Obama ended 'Wet foot-dry foot' the following year. Fidel's brother Raúl, who succeeded him as President, gave way to Miguel Díaz-Canel, although Raúl is chief secretary of the communist party; in other words he's still the boss. Díaz-Canel, who is a lot younger, is a canny politician who may show more liberal behaviour one day, but for now he's concentrating on not offending the powers that be, i.e. not getting fired. Meanwhile, most Cubans are still dirt poor. Many still want to leave and have enough relatives in Florida willing to pay my fees that I stay in business.

Anyway, I was taken to a prison island off the south coast of Cuba and locked in a cage four feet square and three feet high. I was there for three days and suffered the worst pain I've ever experienced.

They were trying to get me to explain why Martin Sanchez-Madera, an opposition political figure, was on my boat. The problem was, I had no idea. He was just a passenger, one of twenty. I couldn't tell them something I didn't know. I would almost certainly have died in that cage.

So, heartfelt thanks to my friend Oliver who

enlisted Bruno, my contact in Havana. That in turn led to Pedro sending a helicopter full of anti-Castro freedom fighters to rescue me.

"You were together at a party last night?" I asked.

"Yes."

"Could that have something to do with this?"

"Maybe."

"What sort of party?"

"It was on Star Island."

"The high rent district, eh?"

"Yep."

"Where exactly?"

"At Stanley Rothman's place."

I formed a mental picture of Rothman, a short, bald businessman in his seventies with a permanent unfriendly smirk.

"Really! Are you party-going buddies with Mr. Rothman?"

Who is Stanley Rothman? He's the owner of the huge Portofino Resort in Las Vegas and its even bigger counterpart in Macau. So he is very rich. He's also a nasty piece of work. He tried to open a casino in Havana a couple of years ago by bribing Hector Cruz, a crooked police chief and would-be next president of Cuba. That didn't work out – Cruz came to a sticky end one dark night at the hands of my friend Oliver. Besides that, one of Donald Trump's first actions on becoming president was to tighten the rules against US investment in Cuba that Obama had relaxed.

Pedro looked embarrassed. "No, but I admit I was curious to see his place on the island."

I would have been curious too. You don't buy a home on that man-made rock unless you are really in the chips. Star Island was built by the Army Corps of Engineers in the 1920s and sits in Biscayne Bay, connected to the mainland by a narrow causeway. Movie stars, athletes and wealthy financiers like Rothman live there. It's the polar opposite of my own little island, Coquina Key, which is home mostly to layabouts like me.

"Okay," I said. "We'll gloss over that. Who else was invited?"

"Hannah Mann, who is a good looking doctor from South Beach. Our mutual friend Martin Sanchez-Madera. The rock singer Rod Stirling. Bruno of course. And a couple of British females called Emma and Courtney Watts. Twins."

"That's it?"

"Yeah."

"So apart from you and Bruno, just six people. A select group."

"You could say so."

"Why did Rothman invite them? Not because they were his close friends, I shouldn't think."

In Cuba, Rothman had been on the opposite side from me and my pals. He got involved because, in pursuit of his casino ambitions, he was cultivating Cruz, the cop who kidnapped me.

As for the others: Martin Sanchez-Madera was the anti-Castro intellectual who Cruz had tried to snatch off my boat. He was later imprisoned and would no doubt have been killed if Oliver hadn't blackmailed and then shot Cruz. Soon afterwards, Martin found life in Havana too hot for comfort and, like Bruno, escaped to Miami, deeming survival to be the better part of valour.

"Rod Stirling was probably only there because Rothman is a snob and likes famous names," I said.

Stirling was a household name in the music industry, but by no means an ornament. He had a string of convictions for drug possession, GBH against female fans and tax evasion in the United States, Britain and, for some strange reason, Monaco. Whoever heard of Monaco suing anyone for tax evasion? I didn't know they had any. Taxes, that is. But apparently he lied on his application for residence. All I knew about him was that when a girlfriend took me to a Stirling concert, he arrived an hour late and as high as a kite.

"You may be right," said Pedro. "Martin and I were probably there because Rothman hasn't given up on the Havana casino. He's the sort of guy who likes to keep his friends close and his enemies closer."

"In case they could be useful one day?"

"Exactly."

"What about the women?"

Pedro shrugged. "Hannah Mann is his doctor. The Watts twins may just have been eye candy – their father was a wealthy stockbroker on Antigua."

"Do you think anyone there had it in for Bruno?"

"Rothman himself, maybe. As for the others, I have no way of knowing."

"What did you all talk about?"

"Politics, sports, things like that."

"Sounds pretty blah."

"Really. I was only there a couple of hours, then I split."

I was thinking I should investigate each of the guests. I owed Bruno that. I said so to Pedro.

He looked doubtful. "Don't do anything rash."

"Of course not. Except to cut the heart out of whoever did this." I indicated the body.

He shook his head, warning. I remembered that among other things he was a deputy sheriff in Hialeah.

Pedro is my age, thirty-eight. Although born in Florida, he's Cuban on both sides, the grandson of Hugo Macias, a pillar of the Cuban-American community. Hugo was a colleague of Fidel Castro in the early days, before Fidel's communist tendencies became apparent. After speaking out critically a number of times he was arrested, convicted of betraying the revolution – Fidel's standard charge –

and imprisoned for ten years in one of the vast circular penal towers on Isla de Pinos. Finally released, he escaped to Florida where he became an honoured figure among the Cuban population. Now in his nineties, he is more or less retired from public life, but his grandson Pedro carries on his legacy on behalf of émigrés hoping to return.

Pedro is a complex personality who has put his own stamp on the position. He manages to be a respected public figure – hence the deputy sheriff handle – but at the same time the leader of a secret militia of counter-revolutionaries that train at hidden locations in the Everglades in preparation for the day when they will sweep back to power in Cuba, over the cold dead limbs of the regime.

Rothman would be aware of this, of course. No doubt in his twisted way he hoped to use the acquaintanceship to further his casino ambitions one day, on the principle that 'the enemy of my enemy is my friend.'

That I could understand. But for Rothman to cultivate Bruno was harder to figure.

Pedro looked at his watch. "Time to call the cops."

I shrugged. "I guess so. Will you call Hialeah PD? I know you're a deputy sheriff there."

He shook his head. "No, Miami-Dade. This is serious stuff. And when they arrive, remember we only just got here."

To their credit, the police arrived in five minutes, a pair of them, both in their thirties.

Lieutenant Oliveira was Hispanic, handsome, hair glossy black, skin the colour of her name. She wore plain clothes, at least I assume that's what they were – form-fitting navy pants, white shirt on the tight side with the upper buttons undone, no badges.

Her sergeant companion was called Taylor, according to the tag on his khaki shirt. Hefty belt, bulging holster in polished leather you could see your face in. A scowl. Didn't like playing second banana to a woman, was my guess. Red face, pale skin, his bullet head covered in a tight cowl of ginger hair. He would always have a problem with sunburn in these latitudes.

Oliveira took in the scene, including the body, at a glance. She turned to Pedro. "Who is he?"

"His name is Bruno Pérez, he's a recent immigrant from Cuba. Last year, anyway."

She knelt down and leaned closer to the body. Parts of the newspaper under Bruno's left arm were soaked with blood. I had not noticed before, but the tip of the index finger of his other hand was also bloodstained, as if it had been dipped in red ink. A red mark on the newspaper, if you used your imagination freely, might have described the shape of a crude, five pointed star. The points were not regular, although it was a good effort for a dying man. But it was certainly not obvious, at least not to Oliveira, who shrugged and stood up.

She turned to Pedro again. "How do you come to be here?"

"He's a friend. We were going to have breakfast. I came to pick him up."

"From Hialeah?"

"Yes. I'm an honorary deputy sheriff there." He produced an ID card which she waved away.

"I know who you are, and your family."

"Are you Cuban?" asked Pedro.

"Both parents, yes."

Taylor was staring at me. Suspiciously I thought, but maybe it was his natural expression.

"What about you?"

"What about me?"

"Why are you here?"

"I'm another friend."

"He was in the area," said Pedro.

Taylor seemed to have taken a dislike to me. "What's your name?" he asked.

"Feaver. Kon Feaver."

"What kind of name is that?"

"It's Israeli."

"You Jewish?"

"Israeli."

He looked puzzled and turned to the corpse, studying it as he put on rubber gloves. Feeling around in the pool of bloody matter under Bruno's legs, he got hold of a bullet and held it up.

"Looks like a .38." He stood up. "Are either of you armed?"

Pedro shook his head. I did not.

"Well?" Taylor asked, still looking at me.

Nothing else for it. I produced the Glock. "Different bullets, 9mm. And not fired."

"I wasn't implying anything," he said.

The hell he wasn't. "Of course not," I said.

"You usually walk around armed?"

"Depends how I feel."

"Got a permit?"

I reached in my wallet and produced a dog-eared, much-folded sheet of paper which he held close to his nose. Short sighted but too vain to wear glasses? "This is not the original."

"It's a copy. I keep it to show folk like you."

He sniffed and gave it back.

"We have to process the scene," said Oliveira briskly. She nodded at me. "Leave us your particulars."

Which I did.

I took a last look at the body of Bruno with its ravaged knees.

Then I set out to find his killer.

3

It was not yet noon as I headed for Star Island.

I had no evidence that Bruno's death was in any way connected to Stanley Rothman's party the night before. But I had no leads and nothing to go on, apart from that mark on the newspaper. It was a place to start.

I drove out on MacArthur Causeway and stopped at the Star Island gatehouse where I was inspected by an overweight guard in safari jacket and reflector sunglasses. He frowned at my dusty Jeep.

"What's your business?"

"It's personal," I said and smiled.

"These are private homes."

"But it's a public road," I said.

He scowled. He walked round the Jeep and

photographed the number plate with his mobile phone. I drove in.

Star Island is for the rich – actually, the very rich – and the glitzy in showbusiness, finance and sports. Or anyone else with money. Lots of it. A house with ten bedrooms there is nothing.

You can see many of the homes at their best from the ocean. Rothman's place was a white, many-pillared mansion with a huge pool, liberally dressed with tall palms and colourful bougainvillea, but from the road all I could see was fifty yards of high white wall, split in the middle by another gatehouse. Either Star Island folk were obsessed with security or they just liked to show off. No human being here, just a camera, a microphone and a buzzer, which I pressed.

"Yes?" A female voice.

"Here to see Mr. Rothman."

"Who are you?"

"Kon Feaver."

"Do you have an appointment?"

"No."

"Does he know you?"

"He should."

"What's it about?"

"That's enough. Tell him I'm here."

"Just a minute."

She came back. "He'll see you." She didn't sound happy but the white painted boom swung up and I was in.

He was standing out on a long white marble-paved terrace, facing the ocean but glassed-in and air conditioned to 72 degrees. I approached. He did not offer to shake hands.

We had never met but we knew about each other. When Pedro and his troops rescued me from the prison island, it had been necessary for Oliver Steele to shoot the police chief of Santa Clara province, Hector Cruz. This was the same Cruz to whom Rothman paid a couple of million bucks in the hope of gaining a casino concession. Small change for a billionaire, but enough for him to view me with serious hostility, since I had been prominent in screwing up his plans. As we stood face to face now, that may have been on both our minds.

"I'm quite busy," he said.

He was in his seventies, short, a few wisps of ginger hair left. Not a nice face, smooth and fleshy, the mouth turned down, the eyes narrow and calculating. He wore a grey jacket, white shirt and blue tie, the jacket one-buttoned across a prominent belly. He looked overdressed for Miami in August. Feeling the cold?

I said, "It's about Bruno Pérez."

He nodded. "He was here yesterday."

"He's dead," I said.

A flicker of the eyes. Surprise. But was it surprise that Bruno was dead, or surprise that I knew he was dead?

"What happened?"

"He was shot. Kneecapped in both legs, then shot in the chest."

"That's awful," he said.

"You had a party here last night," I said.

A mask came down. Almost imperceptibly, but I noticed

"What of it?"

"Including several Cubans."

"Yes."

"Why?"

"Why not?"

"You didn't invite me," I said.

He looked me up and down. I got the impression that if I'd been a palmetto bug he would have squashed me underfoot. I could see I wasn't going to get much help.

"I know who you are, but you are not relevant to my plans for Cuba," he said.

"Which plans?"

"You know very well. They haven't changed."

"Was that the reason for the party? You were just keeping in touch with people who might one day help you?"

"Exactly."

"But Bruno would never help you, considering how you treated each other." Bruno's efforts had led to Rothman being forced to abandon his Cuban ambitions, at least temporarily.

Rothman gave the slightest of shrugs. It could

have meant, "Yes but one never knows," or "Yes but I thought I could bribe him to change his mind." Or, "Yes so I had him killed."

I heard a voice behind me. "Why don't you throw the jerk out, Stan?"

I turned. The face was familiar. It was thin, fox like and pimpled, the voice gravelly, the whole package bereft of empathy. Rod Stirling, none other, veteran of a thousand concerts and TV screens.

I walked towards him. I don't control my temper as well as I should. I can't help it. It's a trait that made me a successful athlete when I was younger – including playing goalkeeper for Tel Aviv – but it does get me into a lot of trouble, and that included now. I stopped when my face was a foot from his.

"You were saying?" I asked.

Stirling didn't back away. He was tall and skinny, about my age, an amused smirk on his face. No physical coward, then.

"You don't look like you belong here," he said.

"And you do? How's that?"

"How's that? I guess it's about money," he said.

"Which you have?"

"Enough to buy you out a hundred times."

"Well whoopidoo," I said.

He looked me up and down. I was in the clothes I wear every day in the Keys, faded jeans and a navy polo shirt because it doesn't show the dirt, so I suppose I didn't look very smart. I'm seriously suntanned, not a fancy pool-side tan, more the kind you get from working on a wooden deck, painting the cabin, fishing, gardening and all around exposure to the glare of the sun that bleaches the Conch Republic. Add matted black hair and two days worth of stubble and I suppose I could be mistaken for a penniless Latino day labourer.

"What's your name?" he asked.

"Feaver."

"What kind of name is that?"

"It's an anglicisation of Feinberg."

"You Jewish?"

"Israeli."

Stanley Rothman held up a hand as if to stop teenage kids arguing. "Mr. Feaver brought me some bad news," he said. "Bruno Pérez is dead."

I was watching Stirling's face. No reaction. He didn't blink, literally or metaphorically. I wondered if he was stoned.

"Bruno who?" asked Stirling.

"The man that was here last night."

"The small time Cuban wheeler-dealer?"

I didn't like the characterisation but it was basically true. Bruno made a living importing US consumer goods, toasters and microwaves, to Havana and selling them on the black market at a huge markup. Last year he quit Cuba because the pressure was on, thanks to his helping me get out of jail. Now he ran the same business from Miami, dealing with a cousin in Havana and another man in Santiago de Cuba. I assume he was making good money.

I turned to Rothman. "To the point," I said. "Do either of you have any idea who would have killed Bruno?"

Rothman shook his head. "A business enemy perhaps?"

I had to admit it was possible. Bruno's business ethics were elastic and he could have pissed off any number of suppliers to whom he owed money. Customers not so much, since he invariably demanded payment in advance.

Stirling chose to take my question personally. He swayed closer – he was definitely high on something, barely in control of his limbs. "You calling one of us a murderer?" he said.

"If the cap fits."

He drew back an arm and swung at me. I didn't think he could do me much harm so I barely moved, and his fist grazed my cheek. There was a gold ring on his finger and it broke the skin. The sting was sharp.

I guess I was humiliated that he made contact. Anyway, I snapped. I punched him hard on the nose and he went down like a log, collapsing on the white marble. There was quite a lot of blood. I stepped back, embarrassed, and turned to Rothman.

"I don't rate your taste in friends," I said.

He was as surprised as I was and said nothing.

I shrugged and turned to leave. The atmosphere had gone downhill and there didn't seem much point in staying.

On the outward lane through the gatehouse there was another wooden crossbar. The way I felt, I was prepared to smash through it, but luckily it was on some kind of automatic switch and it rose as the Jeep approached.

So much for Star Island. Time to try my luck with another party guest.

Something less violent seemed in order. I decided on Doctor Hannah Mann.

4

I googled Hannah Mann on my iPhone and found a listing for *H. Mann, MD Inc.* with an address on Brickell, downtown Miami's main drag.

I toyed with the idea of calling ahead and making an appointment. My unannounced meeting with Stanley Rothman had ended in violence, after all. Then I thought, well maybe not. That meeting had taught me quite a bit about Rothman and his unlovable pal Stirling. And to be honest, I sort of enjoyed the confrontation. The same approach might work again. So I decided to forge ahead.

More precisely, when I got to her building I took the Jeep to the 36th floor. Yes you heard right, there was no parking on the street. I just drove the automobile onto something called the 'Vehicle

Elevator,' pressed a button and up I went, car and all.

I'd read about these ultra-expensive towers where your ride occupies a garage on the same floor as your apartment, but this was the first time I had been in one. It was an eerie, weightless feeling. My first thought was the expense – it must be costing someone an arm and a leg.

At the 36th floor I got out of the Jeep and found myself facing a glass wall with a door that slid silently back to reveal a lobby and a male receptionist behind a long glass desk. Behind him, a floor-to-ceiling window looked out across blue ocean and farther away the green vegetation of Key Biscayne. The general impression was of light and space.

The man behind the desk was slim, smiling and completely bald. And erotic. I am not into the gay thing, personally. Ever since I began to take an interest in sex I've preferred women. To each his own, I guess. He had an aura though, no doubt about it. Maybe it was the maroon paisley silk shirt open to the waist over a smooth tanned chest, or the vee shaped torso and small buns in tight white pants.

He smiled agreeably.

"Is the doctor in?" I asked.

People sometimes lie or are at least evasive when asked that question. They say something along the lines of she's "in a meeting" or "not available." But not a bit of it, the smile widened.

"Sure, Mr. Kon Feaver," he said with a faint accent. Most accents you hear in Miami are Latino or Hispanic or whatever term you want to use. People call it the capital of South America. But this accent was different, more European.

"Have we met?" I asked. "How do you know my name?"

He laughed. "Pedro Macias vouched for you."

"What do you mean, 'vouched?'"

"He said you would be getting in touch."

That darned Pedro. My chain of thought was interrupted by the appearance in the doorway of a woman who had to be Hannah.

She too was smiling. "Hi Kon!" she said to me, and to him, "Hold my calls, Rudi."

So, German? She beckoned me into her office.

I should be so lucky, to have such a doctor. Blonde, five foot seven or eight, curved in the right places, in a knitted yellow silk dress that fit like paint. And she seemed genuinely pleased to see me. You know how sometimes at a party you'll see a woman across the room who you'd really like to get to know, and it turns out she's inextricably married to some loser and you spend the next week wishing life had dealt the pack better and she had fallen into your lap instead of his? Well here she was, talking to me. I forgave Pedro in a moment.

"So you heard from my buddy Pedro?" I said.

Her smile faded. "Yes, and he gave me the sad news. My sympathies, what a dreadful thing! I gather Bruno was a good friend of yours?"

I nodded. "How well did you know him?"

"Not well. We met for the first time at Stan Rothman's last night."

"I'm trying to figure out the reason for that get-together," I said.

She smiled. "I can't help you there because I've been wondering the same thing."

"Just social, then?"

She shook her head. "There's no such thing with Stan. He has a motive for everything."

"Usually financial?"

"Always financial."

I nodded. "I've been looking at the list of guests and trying to make sense of it. There were some allies and then there were also enemies of Rothman, if you want to put it like that."

"Which are you?"

"I wasn't there."

"The question still applies. Which are you?"

"Enemy, I guess you'd have to say."

"How come?"

"How much do you know?"

She wrinkled her brow. "Not much."

"Well, we crossed paths in Cuba last year. I was running a boatload of folk from Cuba to the Keys – I do that for a living. Bruno was my contact in

Havana, his job being to assemble the refugees and bring them to a remote beach fifty miles from the city.

"The weather that night was favourable – calm, with a full moon. There were women and children and I was loading them onto the boat, using a rubber raft to get them across from the sand when all hell broke loose. The police arrived in force, and a coastguard boat with searchlights."

"Sounds scary."

"Averagely so. The entire boatload was arrested including me, but with one exception, namely Martin Sanchez-Madera."

"There was a Martin at the party last night," she said.

"Same guy."

"He seemed nice."

"He is. He's also an enemy of the regime."

"The Castros?"

"And their system, which is still entrenched. Fidel died aged ninety but his brother Raúl, who is eighty-seven, was President and is still secretary of the Communist party, the real centre of power."

"Sounds like there was a tipoff that Martin was on the boat," she said.

"Yes, and it was not a leak from me because until that night I had never heard of the guy."

"You say he escaped?"

"Right. He ran like hell into the dunes and they lost him, despite the searchlights."

"How come he's in Miami now?"

"Things were impossible for him in Cuba. He would have liked to stay – he was a professor of Political Science at the university in Havana and a candidate for leadership when the regime finally comes to an end, but he grabbed a ride on another boat and got out. He works in Miami now. He has a job lecturing at UM. They haven't made him a full professor but he's very much in demand, understandably given his experience."

"We talked a bit. He seems smart," she said.

"He is."

She tossed her head and her blonde hair kissed her shoulders. "So the good guys at the party include him and me – and Bruno of course. As for bad guys, you'd have to include Rothman himself. Who does that leave as unknowns? I guess Rod Stirling and the Watts girls."

"You can put Stirling in with the baddies," I said.

"Why?"

I thought about my exchange with the singer that morning. "Trust me. Tell me about the Watts girls. Who are they?"

She smiled. "Twin sisters, British, plenty of money."

"What are they doing in Florida?"

"I'm not sure. Their father was a stockbroker or money manager, something like that, into offshore bank accounts and such. That's where the money comes from. They have a big house in Cocoplum."

Cocoplum is an expensive subdivision in Coral Gables. "Is their father based in Miami?"

"He died several years ago. And it's Antigua, he ran a hedge fund on Antigua."

"The girls inherited?"

"So I understand."

I scratched my chin. Realised I hadn't shaved. My five o'clock shadow starts around noon. "I guess I should pay them a visit, too."

She looked at me appraisingly. "They are good looking."

"Both of them?"

She nodded. "Identical twins."

I was out of questions. I got up to leave.

"What sort of medicine do you practice?" I asked.

She smiled. "Whole body health."

"Is that a specialty?" I asked.

"It is here."

"Sounds a bit vague. Is it covered by insurance?"

"Maybe. But I only deal with rich patients, frankly."

"It seems to provide a good living." I looked around the room, and out of the panoramic window across towards Key Biscayne. The distant Key was lapped by blue water and my view was framed by the reds, greens and yellows of downtown Miami's high-rise buildings. Miami is a colourful city, literally. When the drug boom hit in the days of Miami Vice and pastel linen suits, big money, much of it from offshore, went into transforming the look of the city with brightly coloured buildings. It's one big Mondrian canvas.

She laughed. "Yes, and I'm not ashamed of it." She looked at me closely. "I doubt if you need my services, though, you look pretty fit."

"I think so too," I said. "But you're the expert."

"I'm a connoisseur of bodies and I like the general impression," she said.

"Thank you, ma'am."

"What are you, five eleven?"

I shook my head. "Six foot. People think I'm shorter because I have broad shoulders."

"Weight two hundred?"

"Soaking wet."

"Do you diet?"

"No. I eat a lot of black beans and rice – *Moros y Christianos.*"

"You're on the dark side. Swarthy in fact. And that suntan is cool. I'm not getting a clue from your name, are you Hispanic?"

I smiled and shook my head.

"Jewish?"

"Israeli," I said.

"Is there a difference?"

"It depends," I said. I was starting to feel self-conscious.

As I turned to leave she stretched out a hand and stroked my cheek with one finger, then leaned in and kissed me gently on the mouth.

I inhaled a faint whiff of scent. I don't know perfumes but I'm pretty sure hers was expensive.

Hmm. Two choices presented, maybe three: One, recoil. Not my style. Besides, it was a good kiss, so that choice was declined. Two, respond, slightly or wholeheartedly. That was tempting. The third choice was to smile enigmatically and file the incident away for future reference, which is what I chose to do.

A small voice said, "Go for it, you could become good friends fast," but a second small voice, more insistent, whispered, "You don't know this woman, you only just met."

"Does that matter?" asked the first voice.

It might. She had called herself one of the good guys which she probably was, but what if . . .? I don't know if my smile was enigmatic or just goofy but for better or worse I flashed it, turned, and was back in the Jeep in moments, sinking rapidly in the vehicle elevator.

5

From downtown I drove west through "Calle Ocho," the Cuban area along S.W. 8th Street. It's a seedy quarter on the whole, buildings dusty and in need of paint. But at this moment it was preferable to downtown Miami for the simple reason that there were places I could stop and park without getting a ticket.

Going down my list, I still needed to visit Martin Sanchez-Madera and also the Watts twins. My interest in the twins had been piqued by Hannah's remarks, so I moved them up above Sanchez-Madera in the batting order.

Meanwhile, I had a bone to pick with my friend Pedro. I phoned him.

"Hey," I said.

"Hey," he answered. "Where are you?"

"Oh, cruising."

"What are you up to?"

"What exactly have you been saying about me, and to whom?"

"Specifically?"

"Hannah Mann."

"Oh, her."

"Yes, her."

He laughed, embarrassed I thought. "I figured she would be one of the people you would want to see, so I took the liberty of calling her. Just to pave the way. Did I do wrong?"

I waited long enough to convey a hint of disapproval. "That was actually my second port of call."

"What was the first?"

"Stanley Rothman. And Rod Stirling who happened to be there too."

"Stirling was at Rothman's place again? Interesting."

"Isn't it."

"What did you talk about?"

"Not much. I broke Stirling's nose."

Silence on the line.

"I didn't plan it," I said. "He provoked me."

More silence. Finally, "I was afraid your personality might clash with some of these high-ego individuals. But watch out for Stirling."

"In what way?"

"He's litigious, he likes to sue people for large amounts of money."

That particular threat did not worry me for one simple reason: I have no assets. A money judgement against me is worth precisely zero, so anyone who sues me is wasting their time.

The reason is complicated. It has to do with a certain investor, a Wall Street wizard called Carlton Tisch who, surprisingly, is a longtime friend. Carlton's business is in commercial lending, a conventional enough field, but he also gets involved in some sketchy ventures that he would rather not be officially linked to, and for whose debts he doesn't wish to be liable.

No, not brothels, but he does have stakes in bars, gambling websites and import-export to countries that Uncle Sam frowns on. For some of these he needs a sort of pseudo-owner, someone he can trust absolutely and who is willing to be on the hook for any financial claims. That's me. I'm a director of a bunch of corporations whose names I don't even know.

Why me? Well, Carlton is much older than me, but he and my father were friends at Goldman Sachs in their younger days. They took separate paths later – Carlton struck out on his own while my dad rose to become a Director of the Israeli Reserve Bank. Needless to say, I'm a disappointment to him.

After I was unfairly kicked out of the Air Force – I showed great ability to pilot an F86 while far over the legal limit, making me, in my opinion, highly qualified, but my superiors just saw me as a drunk – I roamed the world for a bit, first as a mercenary in the Congo and later running my share of grass here in Miami. I stopped dealing pretty quick because I didn't like the company I had to keep, and Carlton, who lives on Tortola in the British Virgin Islands, took pity on me and gave me a job looking after his boat.

I have off-and-on dealings now with Carlton, his wife Mimi and the previously mentioned Oliver, a young Brit with a decent brain but a limited sense of humour. I guess I shouldn't carp – he saved my life a couple of times, but that's another story.

Where was I? Oh yes, being libel-proof: Carlton insists I own no assets, so my boat, the plane and the Coquina cabin are all owned by a dummy Panamanian company. Who owns the Panamanian company? Another dummy corp, this one in Liechtenstein I think – he did tell me but I forget.

If I need cash there is fifty grand in twenties in a safe under my bed, an adequate nest-egg for most people. I earn enough to live on with the Cuban-running. Being a softy I only charge a fraction of the going rate but it's enough to meet expenses, pay bills at the Rusty Scupper, my unofficial office on Coquina (food but no liquor, I gave up alcohol a while ago) and live pretty darn well.

That's my financial life in a nutshell. It's why, being officially penniless, I'm not afraid of the litigious Rod Stirling.

Pedro knows most of the above, not the sordid details but he's got the gist.

"Where does Hannah Mann get her money?" I asked Pedro.

"Beats me. From her medical practice I guess."

"I doubt it. That office must cost a cool twenty grand a month."

"Not counting Rudi," said Pedro.

"Right."

A pause.

"Tell me about the Watts twins," I said.

"Courtney and Emma? Cute English kittens, charming but with claws."

"Do you have an interest there?" I asked.

He laughed. "A Latino jock like me? No way. My type doesn't appeal to English roses, thorny or otherwise."

I noted his self-description but did not comment. He is physically strong and can drive a golf ball 250 yards on the fly, which is professional distance, but he's also pretty smart.

"One sister is thorny and the other is not, is that what you're saying?" I asked.

"Right."

"Which is which?" I asked.

"You'll find out soon enough," he said.

"I'm going to head that way now," I said. "Do me a favour?"

"What?"

"Don't call ahead. I like to take sole responsibility for my own screw-ups."

"Got it."

MIAMI HAS some attractive older homes, Spanish classical with whitewashed walls and pink tile roofs. They pre-date the city's rapid growth that came with modern air conditioning in the 1930s.

But Cocoplum is not lovely, in fact it's rather nouveau.

Its houses date from the 1950s – McMansions, big and priced in the millions. Many of them are slab-dull modern on the outside. Inside, they look as if they were designed by frustrated corporate decorators. They boast such essentials as movie theatres and mirror-walled gyms full of exercise machinery.

The Watts residence was less grim than some. It had a restrained, two storey white façade and a garage wide enough for three cars behind its roll-up doors. I parked the Jeep, now seriously dusty, far enough away from the doors to leave room in case a car wanted to leave, and rang the bell.

There was a long delay. I was about to ring again when I made out a moving outline through the frosted glass and the door swung open.

"Hello?" she said.

She wore a white bikini, still wet, and was clutching a small towel, having apparently just got out of the pool. She was good looking, no question. Slim and tanned but not overly so, her blonde hair was dark with water and caught back in a ponytail with a rubber band.

"I'm a friend of Bruno," I said. I couldn't help running an eye over her body. She didn't seem to mind, although she tried to hitch the towel round her waist. It was not equal to the task and she laughed and gave up, using it to pat her arms and shoulders dry. No clue as to whether this was the smooth rose or the prickly one.

"Bruno from last night, of course," she said. "He said you would be in touch. Come in."

No 'who are you?' or 'why are you here?' A strange day was getting stranger.

She led the way through the house and back out to the pool. "Fancy a dip?" She looked me up and down, grinning. "I can find you a suit."

I held up a hand. "You obviously haven't heard. Bruno was shot this morning, or late last night. I'm afraid he's dead." It sounded banal. It's not something you often have to tell people.

Her face froze. The silence lasted minutes. I continued. "Pedro Macias – you know Pedro, right? – called me from Bruno's apartment around nine am I went straight round."

"How ghastly," she said. "Was he alone? What on earth happened?" Her precise British accent rang oddly in the humid Miami air. She sounded like my English friend Oliver, probably went to one of those expensive boarding schools they have.

"He was shot three times, once in each knee and once in the chest." I was deliberately blunt, I wanted to shock her. She turned and walked away. For a moment I thought her bare back signified disapproval. She sat down at a wrought iron table and motioned me to do the same. I sat across from her.

There was a pitcher of iced water and a tumbler on the table. Only one glass but that's okay, I wasn't thirsty. She poured a glass and sipped.

"It's still a mystery," I said. "But it could have something to do with the party you were at last night. Did you say my name came up, by the way?"

"That's right."

"May I ask how?"

"We were talking about his time in Cuba. He said you were locked up in a prison cage."

"Why did he say I should contact you?"

"He said you had a boat."

"Yes, I do."

"He thought you would be willing to make it available."

"You want to go fishing?"

She shook her head. "No. At least, not in that way."

"What, then?"

She looked at me as if trying to decide whether to trust me.

"Have you heard of Stiltsville?" she asked.

"Yes, of course," I said. "You want to go there?"

"Maybe."

"Why?"

Stiltsville is a collection of small cabins on stilts, set in the shallows at the sandy north end of Biscayne Bay about a mile from mainland Miami. Mostly abandoned now, it has a chequered history.

In 1933 towards the end of Prohibition, a guy called Crawfish Eddie built the first shack, on wooden stilts. It was, deliberately, a mile outside the legal boundary of Miami. A social club, the Calvert Club, opened in the late thirties offering gambling. It was enormously popular. Other places of entertainment followed over the years including the Bikini Club – women admitted free if they wore bikinis. Other cabins were added. At its height, Stiltsville had twenty-seven of them.

But Stiltsville was attacked by two major forces over the years, mother nature and the dead hand of officialdom. It was raided regularly by bureaucrats sniffing around for evidence of gambling, drug dealing or other vices.

Over the years, hurricanes destroyed most of the buildings. Hurricane King in 1950 and Hurricane Betsy in 1965 did major damage. Today only seven cabins remain, all uninhabited. They are maintained by a nonprofit body, the Stiltsville Trust, which at least stops them from collapsing.

The place is little more than a curiosity now, its ramshackle structures a souvenir of pioneering days. Boat tours go there occasionally, but the visitors do not land. It makes a poignant contrast with the glass and steel peaks of today's Miami.

She did not answer so I asked, "Why do you want to go there? I've sailed past it, there's not much to see, just a bunch of shacks."

"You'll think me very rude, but I'd rather not say," she said.

"That's okay, it's none of my business. How about tomorrow around lunch time?"

She shook her head.

"What, then?"

"It will need to be at night," she said.

"You mean after dark?"

She nodded.

"The boat's at my cabin down on Coquina Key," I said.

"That's no problem."

I thought about asking 'So, when?' I waited, but that didn't yield any result. She seemed to drift away from the subject.

I looked around the patio, taking in the sparkling pool and the tennis court beyond. Beside the pool was an expanse of green lawn, neatly mown and well-watered.

There was no-one else around. "Is your sister here?" I asked.

She shook her head. "Why?"

"No reason. I've heard that you're identical. Just wanted to judge for myself." It sounded crass so I laughed but she didn't take offence.

"We are," she said. "Physically. But temperamentally, that's another matter."

"Tell me more," I said.

"My sister is the straight laced one. Well brought up, conservatively dressed. Boring."

"That's not very kind," I said. She shrugged

"How does one tell you apart?"

"One of us is a real blonde, the other not."

I stared at her smooth stomach, gold above the white bikini. I couldn't help it. But I managed to keep my gaze above waist level. Years ago, in Paris, I was taken to the Crazy Horse Saloon which had a saucy floorshow catering to tourists from the city's five-star hotels. In the musical accompaniment to one of the acts, each verse ended with the refrain "But my neighbour is a real blonde." It's stuck in my mind all these years.

I couldn't reconcile Emma Watts's English voice and manners with the idea. But she was looking me straight in the eye and I admit I blushed.

She laughed. In that moment I felt we were close. Maybe too close. I stood up.

"Let me know when you want to go out there."

"Oh, I shall," she said.

6

I don't know much about offshore bank accounts.

But I have a pal who does, I've mentioned him, Oliver Steele. He lives in Coconut Grove – a haven for restless souls.

I dialled him, mobile to mobile. He obviously had my name in his contacts list because he knew who was calling.

"Hi Kon, what's up?" His accent is as British as ever although he's been in the States for years.

"Not much. What're you doing?"

"Getting ready to play squash."

I said, "We should talk. Can you come round?"

"I have to be on court in twenty minutes."

"Must you? This is important."

"Yes, I must. Squash is important to my mental health."

I sighed. "Okay, I guess I'll come to you. Where are you?"

The squash courts were at the Regency hotel on Key Biscayne.

Steele's opponent was a visiting player from California called Bob Mosier who I gathered was in Florida scouting locations for the annual weekend of a prestigious racquet sports club of which he was president. Seemed a decent fellow, genial and not fanatically obsessed with the game like Oliver.

They had finished playing by the time I got there and were sitting in the bleachers.

"Who won?" I asked.

"We had a really good game," said Oliver.

I've known Oliver for some time and have learned to interpret what I'd call his squash-speak pretty well. When he wins, he says, with sickening false modesty, "X had an off day and I just managed to get past him." Which infuriates X of course.

When Oliver loses, on the other hand, he says, "We had a really good game." So I knew things had not gone well. I caught Mosier's eye but he kept a poker face and said nothing. As I said, a decent guy.

Oliver showered and changed and we went and talked in the Regency bar.

"I need your help on something," I said.

"Shoot!"

"Ever hear of a financial wizard based in Antigua, a Britisher, name of Watts?"

"First name?"

"Harry."

"Age?"

"He's dead."

"That's a big help."

"Sorry."

"I'll ask around," he said. "What else do you know about him?"

"He helped people set up private offshore bank accounts."

"Ah." For the first time he sounded interested.

"He had twin daughters, Emma and Courtney, who now live in Cocoplum."

"That's more helpful. Maybe I should meet them both."

"Hold your horses," I said. "Just research for now."

"You're no fun."

"Yes, well."

"I'll make some enquiries." He looked at his watch. "Got to go. I have to take a shoulder of pork out of the oven."

"How come?"

"I'm working on my Cuban cuisine."

" I didn't know you were a fan."

"Yes. I'm entertaining tonight and I plan to serve roast pork, black beans and rice, with *maduros* on the side."

"What's maduros?"

"You really don't know?"

"I'm a gastronomically challenged kibbutznik raised on raw vegetables and carp that tastes of mud."

"Maduros is fried plantains."

I wasn't interested, but I humoured him. "Any good?"

"Delicious. You slice them, toss them in a pan and fry them. The trick is to use plantains that are so ripe they're almost rotten."

"Good to know," I said. I wondered who he planned to entertain. He seems to attract more than his share of good-looking women. "Would that be Kathy?" He has a close relationship, nobody's sure just how close, with Kathy Smith, a blonde tennis-playing chum of Carlton Tisch's wife Mimi.

He sounded wary. "Um no, someone else." He has a roving eye for anything that looks good in a dress – I've even spotted him casting the odd sideways glance at Mimi Tisch who is a former Playboy bunny and seriously eye-worthy in her own right.

What women see in Oliver has always been a mystery to me – true, he's six foot, fair haired and blue eyed. He's moderately athletic – I gather he represented Oxford University at squash, not the vegetable but the racquet sport – but his conversation consists mainly of dry financial musing that must surely bore any red-blooded woman to death.

We left it there. It was a somewhat unsatisfactory conversation but, to be fair, Oliver doesn't let the grass grow under his feet. I knew he'd get back to me, and soon.

7

I saved Martin Sanchez-Madera until last because I knew and liked him. To me, it was unthinkable that he had anything to do with Bruno's death.

But before heading his way I thought I'd take a peek at Stiltsville, just to remind myself what it looked like.

So I drove north from Cocoplum on US1, passing Vizcaya, the Italian Renaissance style mansion built by James Deering of International Harvester fame, now a museum. I swung onto the Rickenbacker Causeway and drove out over the ocean. Veering right at Hobie Island and past the Seaquarium, I drove onto Key Biscayne and down to Bill Baggs State Beach, where the graceful lighthouse stood, tapering and white. I parked, strolled to the edge of the sand and stared out across the waves.

Stiltsville was a mile away across shallow water. The buildings were less dilapidated than I remembered. These were the survivors, of course, the last seven cabins. Enthusiasts operate boat tours from time to time, but mostly the cabins just stand empty. What was behind Emma Watts's request? Why go there at night? I shook my head, climbed into the Jeep and headed back to town.

I had driven about a mile, still on the causeway, when I glanced in the rearview mirror and noticed a vehicle, a black Hummer, keeping pace behind me. Nothing odd there – lots of Hummers in Miami. Don't like them myself, too showy for my taste, and the upkeep must be huge since they get about half a mile to the gallon. But this one was keeping an anally steady hundred yards behind me.

I slowed. It did the same. When I accelerated it followed suit. What to do? What *I* did was wait until I was on the mainland. I drove west for a bit, then turned south on Ponce de Leon, an attractive tree-lined boulevard. I stopped at a light as it turned red, with no traffic between my Jeep and the Hummer behind. So it drew closer and stopped too, having no other option.

Now for the fun. I accelerated, shot the red light and hung a left. Left again, and again, so I came up behind the Hummer. Our positions were now reversed. You don't need a license plate on the front of your car in Florida but you must have one on the back. I have no head for numbers, so I grabbed my phone and photographed the Hummer's license.

Job done? Well, almost. But then, I couldn't resist. I accelerated forward and nudged the back of the Hummer, and not gently. Both vehicles were doing about thirty. It didn't stop. I nudged it again, harder. This was fun. The Hummer's windows were darkened so I couldn't see who was driving but whoever it was, he or she had to be surprised.

Having achieved my purpose, which was to give the driver a good shaking up, I accelerated and headed south towards the Grove, my destination, leaving the Hummer to its devices. Childish, you may think? Absolutely. But regrettably, that's my character – one of the many reasons I'm a small-time soldier of fortune, not a good corporate citizen with a seven figure salary plus options.

MARTIN SANCHEZ-MADERA LIVED on Kumquat Avenue in Coconut Grove. Kumquat is in the South Grove, not the much tonier North Grove. The North Grove is full of small expensive homes whose owners, well-heeled interlopers from up north, surround themselves with bronzed steel sliding gates and high-tech security. In the South Grove, by contrast, the streets meander aimlessly through thick woods. Yards there are lucky to have wooden fences. Parrots fly screeching overhead. The smell of pot lies heavy in the air. More my style.

I hadn't been to his house before – it was freshly painted and in much better shape than its neighbours. I rang the bell.

He opened the door smiling and waved me inside. He was wearing a jacket and tie.

"Place looks cool," I said. "New paint?"

He laughed. "I'm trying to strike a balance between Martin the academic and Martin the politician. So we live in the Grove but we also keep the place clean."

"What's with the threads?"

"I'm lecturing at the University."

"On what?"

"The next century in Cuba."

"You can see that far ahead?"

"Of course not. But the audience is the ACP, the Association of Cuban Patriots. They like to feel they know what the future holds."

"Will you tell them they can return to Cuba one day?"

He held up a hand. "That's a maybe. Besides, many of them wouldn't want to."

"Despite the lure of their own land, the feel of the hallowed soil?"

"Some of them have that attitude, sure. Others are so bitter about the theft of their property by

Fidel that they moved on mentally years ago. Many have been successful here, of course. Miami has become their real home."

"What about you? Will you go back?"

"That's different. I'm a later generation. I am still young and, if God grants me a long life, I would like to spend it in Cuba." He smiled. "Like our mutual friend Bruno, who I think will also end up in Havana."

I shook my head. "You haven't heard? Bruno's dead."

The blood drained from his face.

Martin and I shared a bond. We had both been rescued by Bruno – Martin from imprisonment in the Cienfuegos Police Compound and I from the unspeakable *caja* or cage on the prison island, Cayo Piedra.

"What happened?" he asked.

I told the story. He winced as I described the kneecapping.

"He was at a party at Stanley Rothman's last night," he said.

"That's why I'm here. I'm going the rounds of the people who were there, trying to figure out if anyone may have been involved."

"Any leads?"

"Not really. Some fishy characters but no real suspects."

He nodded. "Yes, a devious bunch. I'm willing

to suspect Rothman of almost anything but I guess murder is near the limit, even for him."

"I'm going down the list, what the lawyers call due diligence."

"Of course. Any questions for me?" He looked at his watch. "I have to leave soon, now in fact. It's a shame, but we can talk later."

"Not really. I assume you haven't had much to do with Bruno lately."

He hesitated. "Right." He went to the door of the living room and called, "Sylvia." Then to me, "Say hi to my wife, she'd love to see you." He got in his car, a Subaru Outback almost as dusty as my Jeep, and drove off.

Sylvia came into the room and gave me a hug. "Nice surprise."

"Likewise," I said. "How do you like life in Florida? How does it compare?"

"With Havana? Good and bad."

"What's the good?"

"Oh, life is much easier. Materially. Better roads, better food."

"Don't you miss Cuban delicacies? Churrasco, flan?"

"That's actually no problem. I can find better Cuban food in Miami than in Cuba. And no ration books here!"

"Is that all that's better?" I asked.

"Of course not. Here we are free. Martin can say

anything he likes. Back there you may get taken away in the middle of the night." She frowned. "It's hard to convey what that means unless you've experienced it."

"I do have some idea," I said. "But there must be things that are worse in Miami, too?"

She laughed. "The bright lights, perhaps. As you probably remember, there's no neon and not many garish advertisements in Cuban cities. The flashiness here gets me down sometimes, it spoils the natural beauty. I suppose you get used to it."

I knew what she meant. One reason I live on Coquina, miles from anywhere, is so that I can enjoy the stars without having them drowned out by city lights.

"Well if that's the only thing." I laughed and got up to leave.

"And some of the stuff Martin gets up to, I guess," she said.

"Really?" I said.

"He's still very political, it's in his blood. Lots of long phone conversations in lowered tones. That hasn't changed since Havana. Sometimes I wish he'd lighten up but I guess it goes with being married to a political geek."

"Conversations with who?" I asked.

She shrugged. "All sorts. Pedro Macias. Bruno. And there are others." She was silent for a while.

"Well, hang in there," I said finally.

She hugged me again. "It's good to see you. You're so . . ." She searched for a word. "So normal."

It was an odd exit note and I was not sure whether to be flattered, but it was also a good moment to leave.

.

8

I phoned Pedro Macias. "We need to talk. Shall I come to your place?"

"No, I'm still down town," he said. "Want to grab an early supper? Let's meet at Versailles."

Versailles is *on* Calle Ocho but not *of* Calle Ocho, it's too smart and too far west. The bustling Cuban diner is always busy and we had to wait in line. I ordered my favourite *vaca frita de pollo* – grilled shredded chicken with onions. Pedro ordered steak and a *Mojito* – white rum, lime juice and soda water with a profuse tangle of green vegetation, generous with the rum. He took a long swig and smacked his lips.

I watched with a certain wistfulness, not to say envy. I knew if I drank the same thing I would love it but it would cause a load of trouble. If you're an alcoholic you know it's the first drink that makes you drunk, meaning that after one drink it's impossible to stop until you've either finished the bottle or collapsed on the floor.

Pedro drained his drink and waved to the waiter for another, then turned to me. "So you've visited all the guests from the party?"

"Almost. Before we talk about that, I need a favour." I showed him the photo of the Hummer's plate. "Can you use your connections to find out who owns this?"

"I could," he said. "It's not something I like to do. Is it important?"

"It could be." I told him the story. I did not stress the bit about bumping the Hummer. Forgot to mention it actually. I didn't want to complicate the narrative. He scrawled the number on a napkin and put it in his pocket.

"Now," he said. "Those guests."

"What about them?"

"What did you find out?"

"Not much. They were all pretty cagey."

"Maybe because they had nothing to hide, none of them were involved."

"It's possible. But the timing is odd."

Pedro shrugged. "Agreed. And it's all we have to go on."

"How was Bruno's business doing?" I asked. "Pretty well, I heard, still exporting plenty of stuff to Cuba for the black market."

Pedro looked thoughtful. "Good. Very good, in fact."

"Did you and he talk much?"

Pedro's second Mojito arrived. He made quite a business of aligning it in front of him on a paper coaster.

"We have done, but not recently." Long pause. "There's something you should know."

"Yes?"

He leaned forward and lowered his voice. Versailles is a noisy place, more of a diner than a restaurant. Sound bounces off the tables and the tile floor, so I could hardly hear what he was saying. "You know that I have something going with a militia group in the Everglades, don't you?"

"The guys that bailed me out on Cayo Piedra? *Águilas Negras*, the Black Eagles? Sure!"

How could I forget? Financed by my billionaire buddy Carlton, Pedro had rented a military helicopter and flown a platoon of young anti-Castro guerrillas from Florida to Cuba where they fought a pitched battle to break me out of jail. I did not know whether the group was still active. And if so, what Pedro's plans for them were.

"Bruno was helping me with that," said Pedro.

"In what way?"

"It's better I don't say. To do with Cuba, obviously."

I scratched my head. "Are you saying Bruno was killed by a Castro sympathiser?"

He shrugged. "It's possible."

"I guess that eliminates the pretty girls who

were there last night – Hannah Mann and the Watts twins."

"Why?"

I shrugged. "It doesn't sound like their kind of thing." I thought for a minute. "Hold on, though. Emma Watts had an odd request." I told Pedro about the British girl's plan about Stiltsville.

"What's going on with that?" he asked.

"I don't know," I said. "She looks great in a bikini but being good-looking doesn't mean she's innocent."

"Are you going to take her there?" he asked.

"I offered, but she sort of backed away from the idea," I said.

"Press the issue," he said. "See what you can find out."

"Maybe," I said. "Another thing. Martin Sanchez-Madera said something that struck me as odd."

"Yes?"

"I asked if he ever talked to Bruno and he said no."

"What's odd about that?"

"Nothing in itself. But after he left I talked to his wife. She mentioned that Martin had a lot of secretive phone conversations with people. One of whom was you."

"Well, that's true," said Pedro. "We're both into Cuban affairs, as you know."

"The other person she mentioned by name was Bruno. She said he and Martin talked yesterday."

"Ah," said Pedro.

"After Martin had said specifically that he did not talk to the guy recently," I added.

"I get it, you don't have to belabour the point."

"Which suggests that Martin and Bruno were up to something political," I said.

"Martin and I are good friends but we also have some differences," said Pedro. "We both want the communists gone, that's a given. But we disagree strongly about how to get it done. I believe in direct action as you know, using force if necessary. He's more subtle, favouring diplomacy." He laughed. "He's a politician, I'm not."

You can say that again, I thought. I said, "What about Bruno? What were his politics?"

Pedro laughed. "He didn't have any. Or rather, he espoused the politics of Bruno. Whatever worked to his benefit, he supported."

"But if Bruno was with you in terms of combating the Communists, then he was opposed to Martin. Enough for Martin to kill him? Doesn't sound right, that's not the Martin I know."

"Me neither," said Pedro. "But you don't have to pull the trigger to be a murderer. Martin is pleasant, but pleasant people can hire folk to do bad stuff."

"I can't believe we're talking about a mutual

friend who we endured major troubles with," I said.

"World's a wicked place," said Pedro looking at his watch.

He insisted on picking up the tab and I didn't object.

9

After lunch with Pedro I headed south towards the Keys.

I was glad to be getting out of Miami, it felt claustrophobic and dirty.

It has its glamorous side, sure, but it's also the kind of place where bad things happen, and frequently, so that they seem to run together, forming a newsreel of bad acts against a backdrop of crooked money and mean-spirited actors. After a few hours there I longed for the solitude of Coquina where the only bad guys were the pelicans who preyed on the fish off my wharf, and I could look up at night and see billions of stars in a clear black sky.

Cruising down US 1, also known as the Overseas Highway, there's not much to see other than sea and sky, but there's plenty of those. As I drove I relaxed. After a few miles I wound down the windows and let salt air swoosh through the Jeep. It was fifty miles to my cabin and getting dark by the time I got there, but by then I was feeling loose and seeing the world from a serener perspective.

Casa Feaver looks from the outside as though even a small breeze would pick it up and toss it over the rainbow. But appearances are deceptive. Its wood sides and shake tiles are actually cladding that conceals concrete block walls and a roof of steel plate. When I built the place five years ago, I consulted the architect who designed my friend Carlton's clifftop villa on Tortola and made it well and truly hurricane-proof. The rebar piles go ten feet deep, through the sandbanks and into the rock. Steel shutters slide across the windows at the touch of a button when hurricanes threaten. An oversized generator provides emergency power. In a couple of recent storms the system stood up to hundred mile an hour winds without missing a beat.

When a hurricane really threatens, officials declare an emergency and call for evacuation. Sensible people obey the call and drive in slow queues of traffic, north to the mainland and the shelters. Sometimes they run out of gas and go crazy. I stay put. Why? Because I'm not sensible. I admit it. I also admit it can get scary in the thick of the storm. The noise is incredible and the waves can reach close to rooftop height. I crouch in my living room feeling like I'm in a submarine without a periscope, but I stay there anyway.

Next to the main cabin, similarly camouflaged and built of the same materials, is the hangar where I keep my plane, an amphibious de Havilland Beaver DHC-2. It's a scrappy little single engine, high wing, lightweight creature built on floats, but with wheels on the floats so that it can take off and touch down on either water or dry land. It's fifty years old but it gets me around the Caribbean as reliably as the day it was built. It is bright red with gold trim like the Jeep. Why? Why not? Red is my colour.

I still felt hungry, so I picked up a double-sized burger with fries and lemonade. When I got home I sat outside on my deck and ate it out of the bag. I was finishing the drink and gazing out to sea when the phone rang. It was Emma, the English twin.

"I've been thinking of you," I said. Well, it was half true.

"Likewise," she said. "When are we going out to Stiltsville?"

"Whenever you want."

"Tonight's good," she said.

I had been planning to call her, but events sometimes take charge and sweep you along. "Okay," I said. "What time?"

"I can be there in an hour," she said.

"Do it."

And she did.

She drove a yellow Jaguar XJS, a low, noisy sports car, with the top down. She parked it on the gravel drive and honked. I went out to greet her and admire the car. She wore a straw panama hat with a scarf tied over it and under her chin. She untied the scarf and gave me the full wattage smile.

"Very British," I said, indicating the car.

"Yes, well," she said.

We sat on the deck and I poured her a beer. Even though I'm a recovering alcoholic I keep some in the fridge for company and yes, it's a temptation. Sometimes I'll get a strong desire to slip and crack one open. I've managed to resist it for ten years. One day at a time.

A few miles across the water, in fading light, we could see Duck Key and the lights of Marathon, population 8,645, which passes for a big city in the Conch Republic.

"It's almost dark," she said. "How long will it take us to get to Stiltsville?"

"About six hours."

She sat up, shocked. "That long?"

"No need to look surprised. It's a hundred miles away. Is that a problem? You said you wanted to get there under cover of darkness, and you will."

"Do we really have to spend six hours sitting in a boat?"

"What a hardship," I said.

She looked cross. "There must be a better way."

There was a discontented silence as she swigged her beer. "Pity we can't fly," she said.

"I do have a plane," I said and nodded towards the hangar.

She brightened. "Why didn't you say so?"

That settled that.

"We have some time to kill," I said. "Even at midnight there will be a lot of light from the city. If you want to be inconspicuous we should not really get there until two am when some of the street-lights will have dimmed. That means leaving here around one o'clock."

She looked at her watch. "It's only nine now, we have time to kill."

I said, "I have some work to do. Can you amuse yourself?"

"No problem."

She stretched languorously. "It's peaceful here. I feel I can relax."

"That's the general idea," I said.

"I feel like a swim," she said.

"I can't lend you a suit."

"Not a problem." She stood up and started peeling off her top.

You've heard the one about not mixing business and pleasure? Normally I regard it as a stuffy and old-fashioned idea but on this occasion I was seriously torn. Emma aced all the usual criteria for a knockout female, but with Bruno's death there was a lot on my mind. So I made a point of walking indoors and sitting at my desk in the corner of the living room. From there I could hear the cheerful splashing sound of Emma cooling off in the Straits of Florida. It was mildly distracting.

A few minutes later, a dripping figure appeared in the doorway. Full frontal, no holding back. The hundred-watt smile again. "That was refreshing." She walked straight up to me, leaned over and wrapped her arms around me. I felt a sloppy wet kiss in the middle of my forehead. She was a real blonde, I had the savoir-faire to notice.

I disengaged gently despite the fact that she seemed interested in a more perfect union.

"When we know each other a bit better," I said.

"Spoilsport."

"Yes, well," I said

She didn't seem upset. Personally, I hate rejection and am in awe of people who handle it well but she seemed to have no problem in that area.

"Got anything to eat? I'm starving," she said.

I looked at my watch. "We've still got a couple of hours. I've eaten, but we could pop round to the Rusty Scupper."

"Sounds like a dive."

"Best joint on Coquina. The only one, come to think."

"How's the food?"

"Great fried shrimp and clams. Onion rings to die for."

"Works for me, but I need a shower," she said.

"I'll get you a towel."

JEAN, bartender/waitress at the Rusty Scupper, is buxom, brunette and thirty, with a lovely smile when she chooses to use it and a nice line in sour disapproval when she doesn't. She and I have a 'best friends and maybe something more' kind of relationship. The 'something more' is intermittent, due to the fact that I consider myself too young at thirty-eight to settle down and she considers me too immature to sustain a serious relationship. Some time ago, when I moved to the area, she was thinking of divorcing her husband, an accountant working for the city government, because he was abusive. She treated me as a trial balloon for a few months before dumping him. Things then cooled off a bit, I think she realised a trial balloon could become a damp squib if you had to live with it twenty-four seven. Which suited me okay and we get on fine now.

But there's still an occasional frisson, whatever that is. Such as when I walk in late at night with a blonde on my arm. Especially a stunner with an English accent.

The place was quiet, half a dozen people dotted around.

"Hi, stranger," said Jean, polishing the bar top. It had been all of a week.

"Table?" I said.

She pointed. "That one okay?"

"Sure."

She brought two huge, laminated menus showing signs of much use, and put one in front of each of us. I knew it by heart and pushed it away. "Just onion rings for me." A guilty treat. "Emma, what's your pleasure?"

"Feel free to take a minute . . . Emma," said Jean sweetly. The faint pause was enough to charge the remark.

Emma flashed a demure version of the hundred watt smile, eying the name badge on Jean's uniformed bosom. "I'll have your fried shrimp and clams and a beer, please. That would be absolutely super...Jean."

The second pause was enough to acknowledge the first, a subtle English 'screw you kid, go fix the food and leave us alone' moment.

Standoff. Jean retreated.

The food arrived and was addressed.

"Shrimp okay?" I asked.

She nodded with her mouth full and smiled.

It was a good opportunity to enquire into her background. I asked, "What brought you to Miami?"

"My father was a stockbroker, you probably knew that."

"I did. Miami's a good place for it I guess, plenty of money around."

"Oh not in Miami, on Antigua. He had an

international practice among high net worth individuals."

"The filthy rich, with yachts?"

She shook her head. "Actually he specialised
more in political refugees. They have a lot of
money too, but they don't flaunt what they have,
they tend to play it close to the vest."

"I get that. A lot of South Americans?"

"Some. And from Cuba."

"Anti-Castro émigrés, folk like Hugo Macias?"

"No, the other side."

"I thought all Cubans were broke – it's a
communist state."

She savoured a clam, washed it down with
Corona, smacked her lips. "That's the official line.
And most are. But you don't really think Fidel was
a pauper, do you?"

"I never thought about it."

She shook her head. "He had a string of resi-
dences, a private island and, thanks to my father's
good offices, hard currency from here to Timbuktu.
Well not Timbuktu, but somewhere else handy, for
sure."

"Why would he bother, he'd hardly need it
considering he lived in luxury in Cuba."

She shrugged. "Maybe it was his Plan B."

"In case things went south politically?"

She nodded.

"But they never did," I said. Fidel had died aged

ninety the year before. "He was at the top of the tree right up to the bitter end."

"That's true, as it turned out."

An idea was starting to dawn in my mediocre brain. I won't say I'm a quick thinker but I get there in the end, particularly where money is involved.

"You say Fidel had millions. Fidel is dead. The question would seem to be, what happened to the millions?"

She dipped a fried clam in tartare sauce and nibbled. "What indeed?"

"Are you saying your father set up Fidel's accounts?"

"He was involved. He was the agent outside Cuba for Castro's financial advisor, and was close to the bank that they used."

"So he would know, right?"

"My father, God rest his soul, also died last year."

"I'm sorry."

"Yep. Lung cancer, smoked like a chimney."

After a respectful pause I asked, "Did he die before or after Fidel?"

"Two weeks after. But he had been in hospital for several weeks in very poor shape."

I looked at my watch. "We'd better make tracks."

I paid the bill. Jean waved goodbye with a neutral, "Have a great evening."

If she only knew.

10

Back at the cabin, I asked Emma, "What happens when we get to Stiltsville? What's your game plan?"

I probably sounded a bit sarcastic. The whole project struck me as sketchy and I somehow expected her to be vague and disorganised about things.

I could not have been more wrong. Suddenly she was all business. She started by changing into tight black jeans, dark green tee and sneakers from a bag in the trunk of the Jag; she had obviously thought carefully about what to wear. Then she produced a chart three feet square and spread it on the kitchen table.

"Here's our destination. There are seven shacks, see, in a diameter of about a hundred yards. I want to land on this one." She stabbed with her thumb on one of the easternmost cabins, on the side farthest from mainland Miami.

"You're looking for something? What? Maybe I can help."

She ignored my offer, rolling up the chart. I persisted. "How much time are you going to need?"

She shrugged. "Not much."

"Well that's good news because the less time we spend tooling around Biscayne Bay the better. Even at two am there is likely to be the occasional cop car cruising around, and if one spots us floating in the shallows it will be time to get the hell out of there. Unless you'd welcome a friendly chat with the law, something you probably want to avoid."

She relented. "You're right, of course. But I won't need long at all. Five minutes should do it."

So we set out. I strapped her into the passenger seat of the Beaver. We taxied away from the cabin and turned our nose towards the north.

The Beaver can take off from water even in a slight swell, but that wasn't necessary as the sea was calm. There was the thinnest of new moons as we built up speed and after five hundred yards, lifted into the air. Five hundred is a generally accepted definition of short takeoff – the Beaver can do it in less and I enjoy trying, but this was not a time for showing off. It's a noisy plane I have to admit, so I fitted her with earphones and mike so that we could talk.

"This is fun," she shouted.

I said nothing.

After about an hour, the lights of Miami tinted the sky ahead of us. I checked my watch – it was almost two am but Miami's an all-night kind of place and things weren't going to get any darker.

I altered course ten degrees east so as to get farther away from land. It was dark out there in the Atlantic, so at least we could approach Stiltsville from obscurity and reduce the chance of being spotted by a casual observer. I wasn't sure why anyone would be looking out for us, but it made sense to be as inconspicuous as possible.

Finally, "Hold tight," I said, and pushed the stick gently down. We descended in a shallow arc from the east, leaving Key Biscayne and the lighthouse on our right and touched down, kissing the water nice and gently, though I say so myself.

"Cool landing," she said.

But now came the difficult part, locating what I had mentally dubbed 'Cabin A.' There were no spotlights or beacons on the cabins; why should there be, with few visitors to speak of and none after dark.

I pointed the plane's headlamp, with the beam dimmed, and teased the aircraft's nose left and right until the beam caught and illuminated a small square structure, little more than a horizontal platform about thirty feet across, on wooden stilts ten feet high. A plain wood cabin with a flat roof and a single window perched at one side of the platform. There was a ladder of sorts attached to one of the stilts.

"That's it, that's the one," she said excitedly.

The plane's motor was idling gently. I gave it a touch of gas and we approached to within about ten feet.

"This is the best I can do," I said. I couldn't get closer without risking damage to the plane.

"How will I get there from here?" she asked, sounding irritated. "Must I swim?"

"You can wade," I said. "The water's barely three feet deep and the bottom is sandy."

She kicked off her sneakers and slid into the water which came up to her waist. In a moment she reached the ladder and swarmed up it. I watched her disappear inside the cabin. She was there for about a minute before she reappeared holding some kind of flat box or package, about twelve inches by eight, in her arms. She shinned down the ladder and began to push her way through gentle ripples towards the 'plane.

She was still six feet away when my ears were assailed by the sound of a power boat and a loud one at that. The scene was flooded with light. The boat was only a hundred yards away and approaching fast. No way to make out its shape behind the floodlight, or know who or what it was. It could be Coastguard, or a casual night sailor, or something more sinister. Whoever it was, they were certainly inquisitive.

"Hurry," I shouted.

"What's happening?" she asked.

"Who knows? Jump on and let's get out of here." I had a strong sense that whoever they were they were not our friends.

She scrambled up on the plane's float, still carrying her package, and I pulled her into the cabin. Thanks to some sixth sense I had kept the Beaver's Pratt & Whitney R985 engine idling the whole time. I gunned it now, turned our nose south-east, away from our new-found friends and accelerated into the gloom.

After takeoff, I leveled off at five hundred feet. I could have headed south for Coquina immediately but I was curious and hung a U-turn, taking us back over Stiltsville, my lights extinguished. I wanted to get a look at the craft that had come up on us.

I swooped low over the area and spotted the boat. From a height of a hundred feet I could see its shape clearly – it was a 'cigarette boat,' one of those long narrow craft built for speed and more at home on the racing circuit. At a glimpse, I'd say a fifty foot Roughrider with a Mercedes engine capable of eighty miles an hour. Not Coastguard, then. I could just about discern two occupants staring up at us from the open cabin, one of them pointing with arm outstretched.

At this point a sensible person would have gained altitude and headed for home. I know a few sensible people, some of them are my good friends, but I am not of their kind. Which is why, like an idiot, I turned and swooped back over the boat as low as I safely could. My floats skimmed the boat at maybe a dozen feet. Why? They annoyed me I guess, so I felt like annoying them back. I wanted to make the folk on board duck, at least.

Big mistake! One of the passengers swung the boat's spotlight away from the shack and aimed it directly up at the Beaver. The glare was dazzling. I had to screw up my eyes and make a major effort to hold my course and speed. The other man's outstretched arm held something, a firearm of some kind, and I was met by a stream of bullets. I suspected a semi-automatic, a Heckler and Koch 416 or similar, only twenty rounds per mag but able to fire all of them in a few seconds.

And we were hit.

The slug zipped through the cabin like a wasp. Only one shot. No idea where it went except it did not hit either of us, thank God. But that was the end of my showing off. I climbed to fifteen hundred feet as fast as I could and headed for home.

"You okay?" I asked.

She laughed. I think she was actually enjoying herself. "Yeah. Wet but safe."

"Try not to get seawater all over my nice cabin," I said.

In response she shrugged off her soaking jeans. She was wearing black underwear. "Better?"

"Much," I said. By now I was getting used to her attitude to deshabille.

"Who do you think that was?" I asked.

"Beats the heck out of me," she said, but there was a pause before her words.

"What's in the package?" I asked.

The pause was longer this time. It stretched out until I realised she wasn't going to answer.

"Okay. Private, I guess," I said.

She laughed and put out a hand and patted my cheek. "Don't take it personally," she said. "You did an amazing job."

By the time we got back to Coquina and climbed out of the Beaver it was starting to get light.

"You can have my bed, I'll take the couch," I said.

She smiled. "You're very kind, but I need to get back. Things to do." She changed into the clothes she had worn on arrival.

"Going to wear the hat?" I asked. She shook her head. "Too chilly."

I helped her put up the fabric top of the Jaguar and she climbed in with a wave and a grin and took off, presumably for Cocoplum, but who knew?

Much to think about. Stiltsville. Castro money. What was in the package?

I have a sophisticated technique for dealing with situations I don't fully understand – I quit. This was such a case. So I did the equivalent; I poured myself a ginger ale, showered, went to bed and slept for a good eight hours.

11

I woke around one pm and stumbled into the kitchen, where I fumbled with frying pan and fridge and managed to fix that good old southern delicacy, bacon, eggs and grits. But minus the grits, which I consider the most tedious pap ever invented by a gastronomically challenged US society. No taste at all. The rest of it went down a treat though, lubricated with Bustelo cappuccino from the Gaggia machine, the only extravagance in my spartan kitchen.

Emma was a conundrum. Something fishy going on, for sure. And speaking of fish, she was not the only one in the sea when it came to finding Bruno's killer. Besides the other party guests there was the crew of the cigarette boat, so the list was growing.

I needed to talk to someone. Whenever I feel that way I tend to head for the Rusty Scupper and share the problem with Jean. It's my office and she's my secretary in a Conch kind of way. I hoped I hadn't queered my pitch the night before by producing Emma, but I didn't think so. We've been through a lot together, Jean and I, some good and some bad, and she's a rock.

I fired up the Jeep and drove round there. She works a split shift, the early part ending at 2 pm, and she usually goes home and rests up until the evening session begins at seven. I got to the Scupper at five minutes of two, parked the jeep and strolled inside. She was just leaving.

"Coffee outside?" I suggested. The Scupper has a few wooden tables on a terrace shaded from the bright sun and occasional downpour by big beach umbrellas. She nodded and we went and sat on the deck overlooking the Atlantic.

"So how was your evening?" She grinned.

"You wouldn't believe," I said. We have very few secrets and I told her about the death of Bruno, my round of visits to possible suspects in Miami, and the jaunt to Stiltsville by night, including the run in with the cigarette boat.

"I've met Bruno," she said thoughtfully. "You brought him here last year. He propositioned me."

She was right. I had forgotten. Bruno was a nice guy but he was always chasing a buck, and a woman. He conceived the idea that I might expand my people-carrying gig to include transporting various consumer goods, notably reconditioned mobile phones, from Florida to Havana. He made it sound an obvious thing to do. "Listen," he said, "your boat is empty on the trip to Havana, right? It only fills up on the return run. So you take the goods down, hand them over to my associate in Havana, and we split the profit."

Like most of Bruno's projects it sounded plausible, but I passed on it for a couple of reasons. First, Bruno's idea of a profit split was usually weighted heavily in his favour. But also it wasn't me. I do the people carrying not just for the dough, but because I dislike the Castro regime and feel sorry for ordinary Cubans. It's not a commercial thing. I don't need more money because I don't spend much and if I do need more I know where to turn – did I mention Carlton?

"I didn't know he propositioned you," I said. "Did you take him up on it?"

She grimaced. "Not my type."

"Anyway," I said, "I still have no idea who killed him. Do you like any of those suspects?"

She looked thoughtful. "From what you say, Emma Watts is a possible. As for the others, I can't say I like the sound of any of them. Stanley Rothman is sordid. Rod Stirling isn't much better. As for the doctor woman, Hannah, that's a weird setup. If I were you I'd take a closer look at her so-called secretary, Rudi. He sounds just the type for some sleazy action."

"I agree," I said.

"By the way," she said, "you said that when you buzzed the cigarette boat they shone a spotlight on your plane."

"Yes."

"Does that mean they can find out who you are?"

I hadn't thought about that, but she was probably right. There were no identifying numerals or letters on the Beaver but a record search would soon identify any DeHavilland DHC-2 registered in South Florida. Still, I doubted that it made much difference to anything. By now, my enquiries about Bruno's death must be common knowledge to any interested parties.

She looked at her watch. "I must go, I have to feed the cat."

"I'll hang out for a while," I said. "Nice and peaceful here, helps me think."

It wasn't peaceful for long.

I sensed footsteps. I was sitting with my back to the restaurant, gazing out to sea. I assumed it was Jean's colleague April, come to police up the dishes and see if I wanted more coffee. I was pondering a refill when I felt a heavy hand on my shoulder, pulling me around.

There were two of them, burly guys each outweighing me by fifty pounds and, from the pallor of their skins, not long in South Florida. Both wore dark suits, white shirts and dark ties which at the Scupper only happens if you are on your way to a funeral.

Speaking of funerals, I didn't like the look on the face of the guy who had grabbed me. He was brown haired, pasty faced and scowling. Broad shouldered and heavy set, borderline fat, maybe forty. I don't like to be touched except by good looking women and he was neither. I moved away and his hand slipped off my shoulder. I swiveled in my chair and faced him. He sat down heavily in the chair next to mine.

"Who the hell are you?" I asked politely.

"Take it easy," he said. "We just want to talk."

"About?"

"For starters, a red DeHavilland Beaver."

"What about it?"

"It's yours, right?"

"What of it?"

"Why was it floating around Biscayne Bay last night?"

"What's that to you?"

He leaned forward. "Look, sonny, you need to keep away from things that don't concern you."

"Says who?"

"Says me."

"No, I mean who sent you? There was some trouble with a cigarette boat last night, that's true. It led to gunfire. I'd like to know who was behind that."

He looked a bit furtive. It told me he had probably been on the boat. He assumed a sort of intense expression as if trying to scare me, and said, "You need to get the message. Keep your nose out of things."

"I think I do get it," I said. "But same question again: who sent you? You don't look like a principal, you look more like hired help, frankly."

The intense expression flickered. I think I annoyed him which was certainly my intention.

His buddy, who had sat down opposite and was watching us in silence, smiled. He was narrower than his friend and six inches taller, so that even sitting down I had to look up at him. His suit was not black but dark grey and well cut.

"Let's not get all excited," he said. He seemed to be enjoying the to and fro. "As to your question, we're not going to tell you that. Just be aware that your behaviour is annoying certain people. You do need to get the message."

"Let me run a few names by you," I said. "Rod Stirling?"

"Good singer," sad Tall Guy. "I have some of his CDs."

"Stanley Rothman?"

Tall Guy shrugged. "The billionaire? Owns the Portofino in Vegas? Big Republican contributor."

He looked uninterested, maybe even amused. So no sale on either of those.

I tried again. "Doctor Hannah Mann?"

He shook his head. "Is that a medical doctor?

Would you recommend her for my next physical?"

"Rudi?" That was a throw at random. For a moment I thought there was a flicker of recognition but it was gone in an instant, could have been my imagination.

"Thing is, a friend of mine is dead," I said. "That affects matters. A lot."

"I heard about that," said Tall Guy. "But he was a small timer, nobody of consequence. No need to get stressed about it."

My face was getting warm. "What part of 'friend' don't you understand," I asked quietly. I had been thinking Tall Guy was the more reasonable of the two but his remark reminded me that a goon in a good suit is still a goon.

Tall Guy shrugged. "There's collateral damage in any project."

"So what's the project?"

He frowned but said nothing. Maybe he thought he had spoken out of turn.

Fat Guy interrupted. "Look, pal, here's what'll happen if you don't get out of our hair." He reached under his jacket, inside the belt of his pants and produced a small, flat 9 millimetre automatic. "One day soon, someone – it could be me – will pay you a call and you'll end up dead meat like your friend Bruno. I guarantee it." He waved the gun at my nose, close to my face.

Which, I could have told him, was a mistake. I try to remain serene at all times, but I have my pride and he was making me look a fool in my favourite bar. Granted, there was nobody else around just now, but it was a nice afternoon and someone might overflow from the bar to the patio at any moment.

So I decided not to waste any more time. The fat guy looked strong and heavy. I'm not that big myself but I'm reasonably fit and I have good reactions. You don't get to play representative soccer by being slow. Step one was to swing my fist up sharply against the underside of his arm, the arm with the gun. I guess he wasn't expecting a physical response – I don't know why not, he was being quite unpleasant. With my other hand I grabbed his ear and twisted really hard.

He let out a bellow – of surprise rather than pain, I guess nobody had tweaked his ear lately – and tried to re-centre his weapon on my chest, but by then I wasn't there, having leaped out of my chair, sprinted round the table to where he sat, put an arm round his neck from behind, and started to strangle him.

Advantage me. He was still in his chair and it can be tricky to get up when you carry all that weight, especially if someone is throttling you from behind. He flailed his arms, trying to retaliate. Somehow he lost his grip on the automatic which fell clattering on the deck. That took care of not getting shot.

There is a railing round the Scupper's terrace

where it faces the sea, about three feet high. There are probably codes about railing height but they don't pay much heed to those sort of things at the Scupper so it could have been lower. I stood up and hauled on Fat Guy until he stood up. Quite a weight. I didn't ask if he could swim, there wasn't time. I just assumed he could, most people can. I dragged him over to the rail.

With the rail pressing the back of his legs I think he knew which way things were heading, but the knowledge didn't help him. He was just too slow.

"Watch out for sharks," I said, and pushed. I was kidding, there are sharks in that part of the Gulf but most of them are small and harmless to humans. But he had a pretty scared look as he toppled over.

He fell about six feet into the clear sunlit water. His jacket ballooned out making his body look even grosser as he went under. There are always fish scurrying around down there looking for scraps and they scattered as he joined them. One or two – snappers I think they're called – came back and nosed at their new neighbour. He would have to swim about twenty yards to the end of the jetty and the wooden steps that would enable him to climb out and get dry.

I turned to see Tall Guy eying me with a mixture of appreciation and apprehension.

"Well aren't *you* the scrapper," he said. He

looked down. I followed his gaze – Fat Guy's automatic was a couple of feet from Tall Guy's feet and he was moving to pick it up. It took another turn of speed for me to leap forward, kick it away and pick it up myself.

"Where does that leave us?" he said, still smiling.

"I didn't appreciate what you said about Bruno," I said. Collateral damage indeed.

"Car keys?" I said, training the automatic on his midriff.

He shrugged and reached in his pocket.

"Put them on the table!"

He did so. I picked them up and tossed them into the sea.

His smile faded. "You shouldn't have done that."

"I got carried away," I said. "Guess you'll have to fetch them."

He moved towards me. I fired, a single shot. It whistled past his shoulder, a deliberate miss but it got his attention. He stopped short. I stepped aside. "You can keep on going," I said.

So he too went for a swim. I was sorry about the grey suit but it ought to clean up okay.

I tossed the gun in after him. He could go diving for it if he wanted. I strolled back to my car and drove home. Two more friends not made, but I have to say, the whole episode made me feel pretty good.

12

Back at the cabin I checked my email – nothing there – then went and sat on the terrace.

The afternoon sun was warming my forehead. What next, I wondered. I hadn't gleaned much from my run-in with the goons at the Rusty Scupper. Except perhaps the thing about Rudi, which was an outside chance at best.

No better idea presented itself so I called Dr. Hannah Mann's office. I got Rudi who put me through to the doctor.

"Hi again," she said. Friendly enough.

"I think I need some whole body health."

If she was surprised she didn't show it. She just laughed. "When can you come in?"

"When's good for you?" I asked.

"For you, any time."

"Tomorrow?"

"Sure. But I have to be across town for a lunch. How about three pm?"

"You've got it," I said. But three pm was not what I had in mind.

NEXT DAY I arrived at her office at 2:30, not three o'clock.

"Hi, Sailor!" said Rudi.

"Here to see the doc," I said.

He looked at his watch. "Didn't we say three o'clock?"

I looked at mine. "Rats, got the time wrong."

"Never mind dear, it'll be just us chickens for a while. Get you a soda?"

We sat and sipped drinks.

"You're from Germany?" I asked.

"Austria."

"What brought you over here?"

He shrugged. "Land of opportunity and all that."

"How did you meet Dr. Mann?"

"Hannah? Oh, we have some shared interests."

"Such as?"

"We both collect guns."

Hmm, straight into sensitive territory. Did he realise that, or was he just naïve?

I thought about the shots last night. "Rifles?"

He shook his head. "No. I actually collect pistols."

"What do you have?"

He warmed up. "My latest is a Smith and Wesson 500 Magnum."

I'm a 9 millimetre person myself, but I know enough about the heavy stuff to understand what he was talking about. The S&W 500 is a massive revolver, in fact it's the largest gauge handgun on the market. It was introduced, according to reports, so that the makers could claim exactly that. The slug is half an inch in diameter. In metric language, 1.25 centimeters. It makes Clint Eastwood's 44 Magnum in 'Dirty Harry' look like a toy. It's supposedly big enough to take care of any sporting game on earth. I'm not sure if that includes elephants and rhinos – seems a bit weird to hunt big game with a pistol, but who knows?

He opened his wallet and, like a good American husband showing off photos of his wife and kids, extracted a photo. It was the S&W, an ugly thing with a long barrel. Not the sort of toy you would carry around in your pants pocket.

"What do you do with your guns?" I asked.

"I display them, in my apartment. Sometimes I go to the range and fire them. Fifty weapons and I have permits for all of them."

He put the photo away. There was silence for a moment. I was running out of conversation. The computer screen on his desk flickered, lighting his face. "What are you working on?" I asked.

"Oh, nothing. Routine admin," he said quickly. He tapped the keyboard and the screen died.

The door to the suite opened and in walked Hannah. She looked smart and businesslike in a formal skirt and jacket with a single strand of pearls, her fair hair elegantly up, showing her neck and shoulders to advantage.

"Hi." She slung her briefcase on the desk. "Am I late or are you early?"

"I was early. Just chatting here."

"I need five minutes in my office with Rudi to take care of some stuff, then we can talk."

"No problem." I waited until Rudi followed her into her office. I knew I shouldn't, but when they were both out of sight I tapped the keyboard on his desk and the computer screen came to life.

He had been looking at a bank statement. The name at the top said "Royal Bank of Canada – Belize City, Belize." The currency was US dollars. There were half a dozen deposits in the current month, none for less than a million.

There's nothing illegal or even immoral about having a lot of money, but this didn't seem to compute. For an investment business or a bank it would have been fine, but a relatively modest medical practice? It also didn't sound like Rudi's personal affairs, unless he was an exceptionally rich medical receptionist.

I moved away from the desk. He was coming back.

"You can go in, she's ready." He smiled.

I sat opposite her desk and she nodded at me.

"So what do you really want?" she said.

"I'm still working on Bruno's killing."

She frowned. "I understand. It was a horrible thing. But I honestly don't know how I can help."

"I reckon there are three possible reasons he was killed: sex, drugs or money," I said.

"No drugs here," she said. "At least, not the kind you mean. I can write you an order for antibiotics or even painkillers, but there's not much else going on."

"I'll take you at your word," I said.

She frowned. "Decent of you."

There was a silence. I let it last. Some people don't like silence and will do anything to break it. How they do that can be interesting.

"There was nothing physical between me and Bruno, in case you were wondering," she said. "We only met for the first time at that party on Star Island the day before he died. I don't work that fast."

"I guess that leaves money," I said.

"Guess so."

I waved a hand in a gesture that encompassed

the office, the suite, the view, and the decor. "This place must cost a bit."

She shrugged. "I make a living."

"How did you get started? It must have needed a stiff initial investment."

"I had a backer."

"May I ask who?"

"No, you may not."

Her smile robbed the reply of offense.

"Just curious," I said.

She said, "You said you needed my services in connection with your health."

I'd forgotten about that but I recovered quickly. "Yes."

"Anything special?"

"I'm okay generally. I sometimes have trouble sleeping." It was true, sort of. Hard to sleep when you spend the night piloting your plane from Coquina to Miami and getting shot at.

"That's the sort of thing we can fix."

"Glad to hear it. Where do we start? Do you want to examine me?"

She wagged a finger. "That comes later. First, I need to know a bit more about you." She pressed a buzzer.

"Rudi, get Mr. Feaver a questionnaire form." She turned to me. "You can sit outside and complete it, then we'll talk."

So I did.

Back in her office, she put on spectacles. They made her look quite severe.

"Let's see. Six feet, two hundred pounds. Your BMI is a bit high."

"BMI?"

"Body Mass Index. It's the ratio of your weight to the square of your height. Yours is 27.1. Anything over 25 is considered overweight."

"Oh, thanks."

"It's a term of art invented by a Belgian statistician in 1850."

"So I'm overweight?"

She shrugged. "Human beings have got fatter since then. Be glad it's not over 38. Then you would be morbidly obese."

"What's yours?" I asked.

She coloured slightly. "Twenty-one."

"Well aren't you the healthy one!"

"I'm in the normal range."

"Good to hear. What else can you tell me about myself?"

"I'd need to examine you for that."

Our eyes met.

I looked at my watch. "Tell you what," I said. "All this analysis is making my head swim and it's five o'clock somewhere. How about we leave young Rudi to hold the fort and repair to a friendly bar?"

"I don't like bars but we could go back to my apartment. I have beer and liquor."

"I don't do alcohol but a soda would be fine."

She raised an eyebrow. "You in AA?"

"Got my ten year chip."

"Good for you."

My Jeep followed her Lexus in a generally eastern direction to South Beach where she parked in the forecourt of a smartly landscaped modern tower. I followed her in and we took the elevator to the top floor.

Her apartment was spare and modern with a lot of light.

"You like to be high," I said.

"Story of my life."

She fixed me a soda and poured herself a glass of wine. We sat on the sofa. She hitched herself closer until our bodies were almost touching.

"Nicer than a bar," she said softly.

I hadn't realised what was happening because the change was gradual, but the relationship was moving from professional to personal to quite intimate.

What's a guy to do? I like to be liked. My mission on behalf of Bruno was serious and I had not forgotten it, but I had slowly been coming to the conclusion that whoever was responsible for his death, it wasn't Hannah. She just didn't seem the type. I strongly suspected she was up to something financially, but beyond that I couldn't see a connection.

She smiled. She still had that formal look with the spectacles but it was at odds with the soft contour of her cheek. I reached forward carefully and removed them.

"We said something about examining you," she said. She put out a hand and gently stroked my chest.

It was all downhill from there.

13

I called Pedro the next morning.

"Getting anywhere?" he asked.

"Not really. A few angles but nothing compelling. What I'd like to do is go back to the scene of the crime, to Bruno's apartment."

"Why?"

"In case anyone – a neighbour perhaps – saw anything."

"Fair enough."

I STOOD on the concrete steps outside the apartment. The grey outdoor stairs and walkway were in shade. The surroundings looked sad and soul-less. Yellow tape was draped across the door. I knew the body had been removed but the police still apparently regarded the place as a crime scene, not available to the likes of me.

There were ways of dealing with that. I recalled that Bruno's bedroom at the back of the apartment faced sideways on to his neighbour.

Last time I was there, looking at the body, the blinds were down. When I pulled them up to let in some light, I noticed the blinds on the neighbouring window were also down. Presumably both neighbours kept them down for the sake of privacy.

A shingle on the neighbour's door said 'Smith.' No clues there. I pressed the bell. It rang, a long chime to the tune of "Dixie." I waited several minutes during which a vision of what to expect ran through my mind.

The vision was essentially of a fat bigot, the kind who lives in a double wide trailer behind a chain link fence, keeps a slavering pit bull and flies the Confederate flag.

There was no pit bull but otherwise I wasn't far wrong. He wore a soiled wife-beater tee shirt under a ratty robe and needed a shower. As he opened the door a reek of stale beer wafted out. A Coors can in his hand suggested he had got a jump on the day.

Rheumy eyes in fifty year old unshaven cheeks looked me up and down. "Yeah?"

Not a great start. Well, give it your best.

"Excuse me, sir, my name is Feaver, I was a friend of your neighbour, Bruno Pérez."

The pale eyes grew colder. "Friend, huh?"

"Yes, sir."

He scratched his stomach. "I knew there would be trouble when he moved in, him being Hispanic. This used to be a white building. Guess I was right."

"Cuban."

"Huh?"

"He was Cuban."

"What I said." His eyes narrowed. "Feaver – what sorta name is that? You Cuban too?"

"No."

"What then?"

"Israeli."

"Jewish, huh?"

"Israeli."

Smith frowned. I sensed that although Israeli was better than Latino it was not by much in his book. I improvised.

"I'm trying to put his affairs in order. He has a sister – a single mom in Cutler Ridge who really needs the assets in his estate. But the police are not being helpful and I can't get in."

"What does that have to do with me?"

"I see there's a window at the back, real close to yours. I wondered if I might get in that way."

He shook his head. "Can't help you, buddy. It's no business of mine."

I reached in my wallet and teased out a fifty dollar bill. I smoothed it between my fingers. Given his condition, his eyes followed Ulysses Grant's image with impressive accuracy.

"She'd *really* appreciate it," I said.

General Grant can be very persuasive. I could almost hear the guy calculating how much beer a fifty would buy. I held out the bill and he snatched it. It vanished into a pocket in his robe, and he stood aside to let me in.

His living room was pretty bare. Cheap furniture and a picture of dogs playing poker. In the bedroom the air was fusty. I ignored the unmade bed, raised the blind and opened the window.

A ledge a foot wide ran the length of the building. It appeared to be the only way I could get from Smith's room to Bruno's. I didn't relish the journey – I don't have a good head for heights and the ledge was enough to give me a serious attack of nerves. The paved courtyard below looked dauntingly hard and there was a lot of distance to cover. A fall could be fatal.

But there was nothing else for it. I took off my shoes, tied them round my neck, and took a deep breath. In stockinged feet, with my back to the wall, I inched out onto the ledge.

It was a hot Florida day. Sweat ran down my face and arms. The windows faced each other at a distance of ten feet and the ledge changed direction twice. I had to negotiate a ninety degree bend each time. At the first corner I pressed the small of my back hard against the brickwork and still almost toppled out into space. I got round, but I was absolutely terrified as I came to the second

bend. The charming Mister Smith had disappeared, so no help from that quarter.

Performing miracles of balance I lurched
towards Bruno's window before finally losing my
footing and falling towards it.

My flailing left hand caught and held the edge
of the lower half of Bruno's window. The building
was several decades old, with wooden push-up
windows. I hauled myself up, white knuckled,
transferred my weight from my left to my right
hand and got myself stood upright on the ledge. At
last, I managed to push the window up and topple
into Bruno's bedroom.

I lay on the floor a while. I have to admit I
needed five minutes of deep breathing to recover.
Finally I started to search the apartment.

I knew the police would have searched it too,
but I had a perspective on Bruno that they didn't.
When I met him in Cuba he was buying and
selling US-made consumer goods to Cubans who
could afford them, Cubans who earned dollars in
the tourist industry. Everything was for cash. Cash
had to be hidden and Bruno was a master of hiding
it. He had a heavy safe for money but also a secret
hiding place in the form of a false bottom to a
drawer, where he kept stuff which was compromising but which he needed frequently, like his
appointment diary.

There was a large wooden desk in his living
room and I opened each drawer in turn. The

bottom right-hand drawer was empty, but sure enough, as I felt it from both above and below I could sense a difference of almost an inch. I slipped a fingernail under the edge and flipped open the false bottom to reveal the contents – some money and a diary. Same old Bruno.

I counted the cash – a couple of thousand in twenties and fifties – and put it back. The police had missed it, but I didn't want to risk muddying the waters by taking it and then being accused of stealing at some point.

I leafed through the diary. He had been meticulous about recording his daily appointments and there were entries, often just initials, on almost every page. After a couple of minutes trying to puzzle out what they all meant, I stuffed it in my pocket to study later.

Now to get out. As I contemplated a return journey along the narrow ledge, my heart sank. I had barely survived last time, the odds on falling into the courtyard below were shortening by the moment.

Motivated by terror, I came up with a better way. I simply strolled to the front door and unlocked it from the inside. I ducked under the yellow tape and was free. I shut the door behind me, and it was as if I was never there. The next cop who turned up might be surprised to find the door was not locked. I could do even better. I slipped inside again, set the lock, exited and slammed the door behind me. Problem solved.

Next order of business: read the diary. I wasn't far from Taurus Steakhouse, a favourite grazing joint of mine, so I ducked in there, ordered a burger and an O'Douls and set to work.

14

I flipped through the diary. It was well thumbed, with appointments on most days. Bruno obviously relied on it to keep his life organised.

I recognised "SR 6 pm," two days ago, as Stanley Rothman's party. "P here 9:00" the following day would be the breakfast with Pedro that never took place. I couldn't make head or tail of the other entries. A few were repetitive and I decided for no special reason to focus on those.

The first was "HM" which could be Hannah Mann. It appeared monthly, each month since the beginning of the year. So Bruno was visiting Hannah regularly. For personal or medical reasons? The regularity suggested professional. I made a mental note and moved on. Another entry appearing several times was "ROX" which meant nothing to me. ROX? Was he interested in rocks –

geology? Or rocks as in jewellery? The last entry was for today, this very afternoon.

I wished I had his laptop, but that was presumably taken away by the police when they searched the apartment. There were address pages at the back of the diary and I looked under R. Sure enough, there was an entry for Roxy and a phone number with a local area code. Nothing ventured nothing gained – I dialed it.

Six rings, then a female voice – a recording: "This is Roxy, but you probably knew that. If we're friends, leave a friendly message. If not, Hi anyway. I'd like to get to know you, here's your chance to make a good first impression. Blessings, Rox."

The accent was southern, slightly breathless. Also gin-soaked and suggestive, or was I imagining that? You devil, Bruno.

"Hi, I said brightly. "This is Kon. Got your number from a guy in a bar. I'm interested, but there's a problem. I don't know where you're located. Call me on this line."

I always feel good after taking decisive action, however dumb, and this could be really dumb. But decisiveness deserved a dessert so I ordered a slice of Key lime pie.

I've heard that Key lime pie is sometimes made with regular limes, not limes from the Keys. How can pie-makers be so cynical? Then again, can anyone really taste the difference? This pie was a ten. It was pale green, not white. I began eating at the sharp end. I was halfway through it when the phone rang.

"Kon, this is Roxy. How ya doin' hon?" The voice was the one on the recording but I sensed a wary edge.

I put on my cheerful voice. "Hi. Got your name somewhere and I'm at a loose end today, know what I mean?"

She melted a bit. "Sure honey, want to come round?"

"Any special time?"

"We're open twenty-four seven, baby."

"Works for me. What's the address?"

"Twenty-one thirty-six, North East 81st Street."

Miami has a crazy street-numbering system but after five years I've just about got it straight. "That's in North Miami, right?"

"Sure is."

Not a great area. Not quite a slum but kind of working-class blah. Low overhead for a house of ill repute.

"Any sign over the door?"

"Look for 'Movies'n Massage.'"

That kind of said it all. "Catchy!"

"Yeah."

"Give me half an hour," I said.

"That's not all we'll give ya."

"Roger that." I rang off.

. . .

'Movies'n Massage' was in a small strip mall. The sign was faded, like the two storey office building that displayed it, and its neighbours to right and left, a pawn shop and some kind of medical office or surgery. I read somewhere that Florida is the centre for scams where innocent individuals have their identity stolen and used to claim social security payments for artificial limbs, which are converted into cash, which then disappears. This looked a possible.

The 'Movies'n Massage' building looked slightly sinister. It had no windows and the door was heavy as if made of sheet metal. It opened when I pressed the buzzer and I entered a narrow hallway with another door in front of me, so that I was imprisoned for a few moments. A video camera winked overhead, recording me I guess. Whoever controlled it must have decided I was non-threatening because the second door swung open and I entered more welcoming surroundings.

Roxy, for it had to be she, smiled in welcome.

"Hi honey, you must be Kon." That husky southern voice again. She was middle-aged and blonde, heavily made up. An off-the-shoulder pink satin dress barely covered her generous bosom but I got the distinct idea her function was managerial, rather than being available one-on-one so to speak.

It was a bit like a small cinema. The movie involved a nubile threesome, a man and two girls who may or may not have been of voting age, copulating energetically to a soundtrack of moans and groans. The auditorium was dim but not dark. There were cushioned sofas for an audience of twenty people. Seated on them were four flimsily dressed women and a man who looked like a customer. He was talking quietly to one of the girls, an oriental. As I watched, he took her hand and they left the room through a door leading, presumably, to bedrooms. Another girl, tall and dark-skinned, appeared through the same door and draped herself on a sofa, her face expressionless, presumably having completed an assignment. So that was the system, with Roxy as manager and cashier, no doubt.

I had not prepared myself for this, but I knew what I wanted which was to determine Bruno's connection to the luscious Roxy. His purpose actually seemed pretty obvious, namely to satisfy his appetites. Not my idea of fun but hey, different strokes. Beyond that, was there anything connecting Roxy to Bruno's death? I couldn't see it, but this was a sleazy milieu and anything was possible.

Roxy looked me up and down. "What's your pleasure, hon? We have some lovely girls. They come in all shapes and sizes, as you can see. Something for everyone, I like to say."

"I can see that."

"Well look around, watch a movie, take your time."

Fair enough. It did not get me anywhere but I sat down. The movie was repetitive and less than absorbing, so it gave me time to think.

But in the next few moments, all bets were off. The door to the bedrooms opened and another woman emerged. Damned if wasn't my recent English chum Emma Watts, in a semi-sheer negligée which seemed to be standard attire for the place.

At first she did not see me, hunched on a sofa in the low light. I glanced around nervously and shrank back even more. Should I greet her, or hide? What to do?

Roxy had left the room, probably only briefly. Discretion won out. I rose, one hand covering my face, and sidled towards the exit, thanking my stars that I was dressed differently than when Emma and I were last together.

But it didn't work. Roxy reappeared, full of unwelcome energy. "Hey, Kon babe, leaving already? Aren't you going to stay and have some fun?"

At the sound of my name – why the heck hadn't I used an alias? – Emma looked up and recognised me immediately. She stood and advanced, grinning broadly. "Well if it isn't Kon, long time no see."

"Do you folks know each other?" asked Roxy.

"We're old friends," said Emma. Her crisp English accent rang like cut glass in the incongruous surroundings. "We're going to spend some quality time, aren't we Kon?" She took my hand and made to lead me towards the bedrooms.

"That's great," said Roxy. She turned to me, her smile a little harder. "That'll be two hundred dollars kid, payment in advance."

Whoops! That was one expense I didn't think Carlton Tisch would approve. "I didn't bring any cash."

"We take Visa and Mastercard."

I shook my head and made for the door, leaving Roxy gaping. "Talk later," I muttered to Emma who waved amiably.

Out in the street I climbed aboard the jeep and headed for home, more than a bit confused about Emma's choice of employment.

15

Back at home I sat on the deck outside my cabin and watched the shadows lengthen. There was warm late afternoon sunshine. The ocean was unusually calm, the water's surface as flat as a glass mirror and undisturbed – even the pelicans had gone off duty for the night.

It was time to take stock. What conclusions had I reached as a result of traipsing around South Florida for several days?

Conclusions? None. Some vague leads, but none worth a whole heck of a lot. A motley collection of people met, some seeming faintly suspicious, others not so much. There was Stanley Rothman, aging, venal and unpleasant, Rod Stirling, younger but likewise. Hannah Mann, a doctor with a fishy medical practice and a camp secretary who dealt in millions. Martin Sanchez-Madera, intensely political and, despite his friendly manner, oddly secretive about who he did or did not associate with. Finally there was Emma the English sex-kitten, connected via her late father to Fidel Castro's fortune and oddly intrigued by Stiltsville.

Whom did I fancy at this point? None of them. And yet Bruno was gone and someone had done it, killed him stone dead.

I was starting to feel hungry. I sighed and went indoors. I didn't feel like driving round to the Scupper so I opened the fridge and inspected the contents. There were a couple of eggs, some ham that had been there for several weeks but smelled okay, and a half finished bag of 'fresh' tomatoes that had been firm a week ago but now looked suspiciously soft. Not too promising. I checked the freezer section and found the leftover half of a Dominos pizza that I had frozen three months ago, pepperoni and anchovy. I put it in the microwave.

As the oven was doing its stuff the phone rang. It was Oliver Steele.

"Glad you called," I said. "Hope you've got good news, this whole deal is driving me nuts."

Oliver laughed. "I don't know how useful it is, but here's what I was able to find out:

I talked to a few folk, and the scuttlebutt is that the late Harry Watts, father of your English twins, was associated with Fidel Castro or rather one of his minions, a cove called Gaspar Gordon."

I pricked up my ears. "The name sounds familiar. Bruno had a contact called Gordon in Santiago. He mentioned him once when we were in a bar."

"Santiago? Why would he be doing business in Chile?"

"Not Santiago in Chile. Santiago de Cuba is the second city in Cuba. It's in Oriente, the eastern part," I said.

"Anyway, Gaspar Gordon had some kind of financial dealings with Fidel at one time. He came to see a banker friend of mine on Tortola in the British Virgins. I chatted with that banker today. He says he and Gordon never reached agreement."

I said, "That's not a connection with Watts."

"Not a direct one. But Gordon may have gone on to talk to Watts, after my man could not help him."

"It's vague."

"Maybe, but it's the best I've been able to come up with so far."

A bell rang on the microwave and I fished out the half pizza. It was limp and barely warm, but when I took a mouthful the taste wasn't too bad.

"Well," I said, "I suppose it's a tenuous link between Bruno (because he did business with Gordon) and Emma (because her late father *may* have had dealings with the guy.) But where do we go next?"

Steele laughed. "I guess the way to see if it helps is to ask Gordon."

I demolished the rest of the anchovy-tinged dough. Three month old pizza is an acquired taste.

"He'll probably deny any connection. I would."

Steele laughed. "You'll have to twist his arm."

"Where can I find him?" I asked.

"Santiago, I guess."

"You mean, go to Cuba?"

"If that's what it takes," said Steele. He sounded pretty casual about the idea, as if it was just a trip to the supermarket.

"I don't think there are regular flights from the States to Cuba nowadays, not since Trump reversed the Obama easing in 2017," I said.

"What kind of passport do you have?" Steele asked.

"Israeli."

"Then you can fly out of Mexico or Canada. It's only U.S. citizens that have a problem."

I still wasn't keen, seeing as my last trip to Cuba resulted in my being locked up in a box with a view to killing me.

"How about you come too?" I asked.

Silence on the line.

"I thought so," I said.

"Hang on," he said. "I'll come, but I want to be sure the guy will be there to talk to us first."

"I don't see how you can be sure of that," I said.

"Here's what I'll do," said Steele. "Bruno used email and had a website. That should yield some clues."

"Can you check that?"

"No, but I bet Halfshaft could."

Ron Halfshaft was an odd character, a young computer wizard from Los Angeles. He had helped me and Steele on several projects, notably in Havana and also in South Africa. He was an unfit young man with a pale face, greasy hair and ill fitting jeans, not a candidate for polite society. But he knew a bit from a byte and could find his way around the Dark Web. He also possessed eidetic memory, which is akin to a photographic memory. Some people say it doesn't exist, but those people never met Ron or watched him clean out the house by counting cards in Las Vegas.

"Give him a call," I said.

"Will do." He rang off.

I washed the pizza down with a cappuccino and felt better. Hadn't really got anywhere but I finally had a feeling of forward motion, as opposed to chasing my tail.

16

After his meal with Kon, Pedro drove back to his home in Hialeah.

Bruno Pérez's death had been dramatic but, beyond that, he started to wonder what it told people about the killer and his motive.

Everything suggested that it had not been a random home invasion. There was nothing about Bruno or his modest apartment that would make that likely. What could have inspired the attack?

Money, sex, revenge? He realised he was replaying the kind of thoughts you had if you watched an Agatha Christie drama. But he didn't know enough about Bruno's private life to speculate which of the three applied, if any.

He recalled the star-shaped bloodstain and thought back to the party on Star Island. He had only talked to Bruno for a few minutes, mostly trivia. They talked about Bruno's business.

He had asked how things were going. Bruno had been drinking and his tongue was loosened.

'Great," he had said. "There's a huge market in Cuba for the stuff I sell. I could treble my business."

"Really? I know about all the tourist dollars, but there must be a limit."

Bruno shook his head. "It's only the United States that boycotts Cuba. Don't forget the rest of the world. For tourists from Europe and everywhere else it's a prime destination. The climate, the beautiful beaches. Music and dancing. Havana is a fascinating city. Even the poverty . . . "

"Yes?"

"This may sound cynical but in a way the poverty adds to the attraction. Visitors can observe it without sharing the suffering."

"You talk of tripling your business. So what's stopping you?" Pedro had asked.

"One needs capital to finance inventory, to cover overhead and promotion."

"Rothman is rich, he could finance you."

Bruno laughed, a little too loud. "Not in a hundred years. The guy hates me. I have a plan, though."

"What kind of plan?"

"I have a colleague in Cuba. He's my representative in the second city, Santiago."

"I know Santiago, my family is from there."

"Of course, I forgot. Most Americans only know

Havana. Anyway, Gaspar may be able to help with financing."

"Gaspar?"

"Gaspar Gordon. He's an older guy, very smart."

"An old Cuban with money?"

Bruno nodded. "He's retired now but he used to advise Fidel with his finances in the old days."

"Advise in what way?"

Bruno looked at Pedro and went quiet, as if he had said too much, the liquor talking, and he suddenly realised it.

Pedro thought back to that evening. Bruno had changed the subject after that, but the name Gaspar Gordon rang a bell with Pedro.

He needed to talk to his grandfather Hugo.

Hugo Macias lived with Pedro. He led a quiet life now. At ninety-one his health was fair for his age. He tried to walk a mile a day, but too much excitement was not good for him. When Pedro approached him, he did not know what to expect and he was surprised when the younger man asked him about his time as Castro's financial advisor in the 1980s.

Hugo knew of his grandson's plans concerning the *Águilas Negras*, the secret militia of several dozen young men who drilled and trained with automatic weapons in the Everglades. He had mixed feelings about that. He himself had mellowed over the years and he didn't believe armed conflict was either practical or proper as a way of bringing democracy to Cuba.

When Castro came to power in 1959 it was in the wake of years of dictatorship and turmoil, under Batista and before. There was little democracy then, and Hugo was philosophical about the chance of introducing it now. The best outcome, he felt, would be a more benevolent one-party government. That, at least, would increase the chances of improving the economy.

"I am frustrated, frankly," said Pedro. "Things have stalled. Nothing is being done to oppose the regime."

"Be patient," said Hugo gently. "Things may go better under Díaz-Canel." He was referring to Raúl Castro's successor as president.

"As party secretary, Raúl is still in charge, you know that," said Pedro.

"He's almost my age, he won't be around much longer."

"Don't believe it," Pedro scoffed. "He's durable, like you."

"Anyway, there's not much to be done about it," said Hugo.

"You don't think so?"

Pedro was thinking assassination. There had been many attempts on the life of Fidel over the years, poison shellfish, exploding cigars and the rest. All failed, but they had been poorly conceived and underfunded. With money and planning, Pedro knew he could do better. Removing Raúl would strengthen Díaz-Canel's influence enormously.

But, more and more, Hugo disapproved of violence. He knew his grandson thought differently; the militia group was evidence of that. But he knew Pedro was short of funds. As long as there was no real money behind the group, he could not act decisively.

Out of nowhere, Pedro asked, "What does the name Gaspar Gordon mean to you?"

"Gaspar was around when I worked with Fidel. Why do you ask?"

Pedro shrugged. "Oh, his name came up." He explained about Bruno.

Hugo did not enlarge on his answer. In fact, he seemed to avoid the subject. *Normal,* Pedro thought, *he doesn't like to relive that era.*

"I think I need to rest," said Hugo.

"Of course," said Pedro. Hugo tired easily. It was his habit to take a siesta after lunch. Pedro watched as he walked slowly to his room and closed the door.

When he was sure Hugo was asleep, Pedro approached the old man's desk and opened the lower filing drawer where Hugo kept papers relating to his years in Cuba. He knew what he was looking for and, sure enough, one of the hanging folders contained a sheaf of papers labeled "Money/Fidel." He teased it open.

As he read, his heart skipped a beat. There was everything necessary to access an account in the name of Pangbourne Plastics at Integrity Bank on Tortola. There were fading handwritten notes from when the account was set up, from which it was clear that the real beneficiary was Fidel Castro. As far as Pedro could see, nothing had changed. There was a model power of attorney of the kind required to withdraw money, and even the password.

He returned the papers, leaving everything undisturbed.

Hugo had a doctor's appointment the next morning. Taking advantage of his absence, Pedro took the papers out of the desk again, went to the local UPS store and made copies of everything. Then he came home and replaced them in Hugo's desk as before.

Then he telephoned Martin Sanchez-Madera.

"We need to talk," he said.

17

M artin Sanchez-Madera took the call.

"Did you read the article about Bruno in the Herald?" Pedro asked.

Martin had not. He didn't read newspapers, he was too busy. He scanned Google News on his mobile phone with his morning coffee and that primed him for the day. He spent most of his time working to advocate peaceful advancement of the Cuban cause, which meant replacing the existing Castro-Communist regime with an elected democracy.

"Kon told me about the shooting, though," he said.

"We need to talk," said Pedro.

"What about?" Martin understood that Pedro and he wanted the same political outcome, but he regarded Pedro as a cowboy with no diplomatic skills, a bull in a china shop likely to retard, not advance, their objective. He honoured the status of Pedro's distinguished grandfather. But he knew and disapproved of Pedro's paramilitary *Águilas Negras* and was wary of getting too close to the energetic grandson.

"About Bruno, and money," said Pedro.

"What about them?"

"I'd rather talk in person."

Martin sighed. He had some time available, but he had meant to spend it drafting another chapter of his memoirs, entitled 'Refugee with Dry Feet,' a reference to the way he had arrived in Florida shortly before the wet foot-dry foot policy was abolished. But he did not want to seem rude.

"You're in Hialeah and I'm in Coconut Grove. What do you suggest?"

"Versailles? It's in between."

"Nah, too noisy. How about 'La Carreta?' Better food, too."

So that's where they met.

La Carreta is across the street from Versailles. It's much lower key. The dining room is darker and quieter and there are tablecloths.

Martin ordered Shrimp Ajillo, shrimps sautéed in garlic sauce with white wine and lemon. Pedro ordered a Media Noche sandwich – pork, ham, Swiss cheese, mustard and pickle on an egg roll, pressed flat and toasted. Martin watched as Pedro, with typical gusto, ordered a *Mojito*, swallowing half of it with his first gulp. He himself drank iced water.

"What's the story," Martin asked. "Do you know who killed Bruno?"

Pedro shook his head. "I don't. But I'm reasonably sure it was about money."

"How so?"

"It's a long story. You know that my grandfather Hugo was financial advisor to Fidel Castro, back in the day?"

"Of course."

"Well," Pedro leaned forward and lowered his voice, "I always knew that he was around when Castro's young brother Rafa set up an offshore account for the president. A personal account, not something shared with his colleagues or the rest of his family."

"That sounds like Fidel. So?"

"The party at Rothman's place the other night jogged my memory."

"Why then, particularly?"

"I looked around the room. There was Rothman, who thinks about nothing but money. There were the Watts twins, whose father I know specialised in offshore bank accounts. Then there was Bruno. I also know that Bruno's rep in Santiago de Cuba, a fellow called Gaspar Gordon, was close financially to Fidel in those days."

"So?"

"Then Bruno is killed. Can't be a coincidence."

Martin's attention was now engaged. "You're leading up to something, but what?"

"So I talked to my grandfather. He confirmed that an account was set up. But here's the thing: I think when Fidel died, the account stayed in place."

"And?"

"In short, my grandfather. . . I know where the account is and I have the password and papers necessary to access it."

He's a poor liar, Martin thought. He wondered what had really passed between the young and the old – now a frail ninety-one – Macias. But if he was right about having access to the account, that could be huge.

"Why are you telling me this?"

Pedro held up his hand, confidingly. "We haven't always seen eye to eye," he said. "But we share the same objective, you and I, to end the present regime."

"True."

"We need to work together."

"There are certainly ways we could explore," said Martin cautiously. "With funds we could set up, in essence, a government in exile. Really promote the idea to the world at large, the United Nations. There are many possibilities."

Pedro nodded enthusiastically. "Yes, you see! I knew I needed your political skills. This could really work!"

"So what do we do next?"

"Not we, *you*."

Martin raised an eyebrow. "Me?"

"Yes. For reasons too complicated to explain, I cannot be the one to access the account. It would – might – cause embarrassment in, er, certain quarters."

So that's it, Martin thought. Chances are, he stole the papers from his grandfather. Now, if he's seen as primary in extracting the money, the old man will smell a rat. So Pedro wants me to be the front man, he's okay with that as long as enough money comes through to him.

Well, he thought, *if we can work things so that I'm the one with my fingers on the purse strings, that would be easy enough to live with.*

He smiled and held out a hand to Pedro.

"I think we have a deal."

18

Ted Petersen stubbed out another cigarette and looked at his watch. It was late afternoon and the journalist was increasingly worried. He had to write a column for the *Miami Herald* by tomorrow night and he was stuck for a subject.

He was proud of the name he had made for himself as a columnist for Miami's leading newspaper, but after almost a year on the job he still found it more taxing than he had expected. Writing was easy enough, but coming up with a catchy topic every week was a lot harder.

He tried doodling on the back of an envelope, sticking a push-pin at random in a map of Florida and a few other tricks that sometimes worked to stimulate his weary brain.

Finally, he grabbed a copy of the *Herald* and

scanned it, beginning on page one, looking for anything that might give him a starting point.

Nothing on the front page looked like column material but on page three, below the fold, a short account of a killing in Coral Gables caught his eye. It described a man shot dead in his own apartment and mentioned the body had been found resting on a copy of the *Herald,* splashed with the victim's blood.

He winced slightly at the picture but he was getting desperate and he could see scope for some gallows humour, possibly enough to sustain reader interest for eight hundred words. The byline was Arthur Pottersman, a *Herald* staff reporter. He knew Pottersman well so he picked up the phone.

"Hey Art, Ted here."

"Hi, Ted."

"Say I read your piece this morning about the dead body bleeding out on the *Herald.*"

Art laughed. "Did they run it?"

"Yep, page three."

"I'm pleasantly surprised. Nothing very memorable apart from that lurid detail. He wasn't famous."

"Who was he?"

"Cuban immigrant, made a living exporting toasters to the island paradise."

"Where did you get the lead?"

"Miami Dade PD."

"They called you? Do they do that?"

"Nah. Other way around. I have a bunch of phone numbers of police contacts that I call regularly, just to see if there's anything going on. They usually shine me off, but sometimes it leads to something."

"Mind if I call your contact?"

There was a pause. "I don't usually do that, Ted."

Ted understood. Being a news reporter was hard work in a highly competitive business. Revealing a source to a fellow journalist was generally not a good idea. Nothing to do with ethics or freedom of the press, everything to do with retaining a competitive edge versus your peers.

"I'm just a lowly columnist desperate for an idea. No plans to get back into the newsroom," Ted joked. He waited.

Art relented. "Call Lieutenant Jane Oliveira. She's a decent soul, she might help you out." He gave the number.

Petersen keyed it into his mobile. "Thanks, Art, I owe you."

"You sure do."

HE DIALLED HER. She picked up on the first ring. "Lt. Oliveira."

"Hi, Lieutenant. Need some help here."

"And you are?"

"Ted Petersen. I'm a writer." Well, he was, sort of. "I'd like to ask you some questions about a killing you just investigated in Coral Gables."

"I already talked to one of your colleagues, Potter I think."

"Pottersman."

"Whatever. What do you want to know?"

"Can we meet and talk about it?"

"Busy day today."

"When do you get off duty?"

"Not so fast, Mr. Petersen."

But one thing you learn as a journalist, he thought, is not to take no for an answer. Most people, however shrewd, don't realise what they are up against when they talk to the press and it was not hard to take advantage of her good nature. She agreed to meet him at six o'clock in the bar of the Intercontinental, a few blocks from Miami-Dade police headquarters in Doral.

He got a nice surprise when he walked into the hotel lounge. After her rather curt telephone manner she was better looking than he expected. Standing at the half empty bar, she was in civilian dress, but the bulky black two way radio on the counter gave her away. Tall and slim, glossy black hair, the white shirt impeccably clean. *Wonder if she does her own ironing,* he mused. He looked for a wedding ring but there was none.

He ordered drinks for both of them, Diet Coke

for her and a margarita for himself. He tried to pay for both drinks but she stopped him and paid for hers.

"It's only six dollars," he said.

"I know, but . . ."

"But what?"

"You know what."

They sipped their drinks in silence.

"You first," she said.

"I write a column in the *Herald.* I'm looking for a subject for tomorrow."

"I know who you are, I looked you up. Where's the subject matter in this?"

"I don't know yet."

"Okay," she said slowly. She smiled for the first time. It was a nice smile and he felt himself falling in love. Stay focused, he told himself.

"Do you have any leads as to the man's killer?" he asked.

She shook her head. "It's early days."

"How did you discover the body?"

"A friend of his phoned us."

"How did the friend discover him?"

"He went to the apartment and there was Pérez, dead."

"Any idea of motive?"

"Nope."

"What was Pérez's job?"

"He was self employed. Some kind of export business according to his friends."

"Friends plural?"

"Two of them."

"Who were they?"

"One was an Israeli guy from the Keys who carried a gun. Claimed he was in transportation. The other was Cuban American, quite well known."

"Who?"

"Name of Pedro Macias."

The name didn't ring a bell with Petersen. "What's he well known for?"

"He's active in politics – opposed to the Cuban regime, needless to say."

"Republican, then."

She shook her head. "Not necessarily. Not every Cuban is that way. The Republican Party argues that they oppose Castro and the Democrats do not, but that's largely a mantra to get votes, Mr. Petersen."

"Ted."

"It's a mantra, Ted."

Besides a pretty face she had a brain. Better and better.

"I'd like to meet Pedro Macias."

"It's a free country. He lives in Hialeah."

"Another Coke?"

She shook her head. "Thanks, but I have to be somewhere."

They strolled towards the street.

"Well thanks, you've been a great help, Lieutenant."

"Jane." The smile again.

"Thank you, Jane."

As he walked to his car he felt unusually cheerful and he knew exactly why.

19

Petersen phoned Pedro Macias.

"I'm doing a series – profiles of influential Miami citizens. Can I come and see you?"

Pedro laughed. "If you think I qualify as influential you can't have a very high opinion of the other guys."

"You sell yourself short," said Petersen.

"It's your gasoline. Come on by."

HE DROVE TO HIALEAH.

The Macias home was on the edge of a golf course, overlooking the third fairway. It was a large ranch-style house in the Spanish style, with white walls and pink tile roof. Pedro poured him a glass of wine and they sat in the comfortable lounge, nursing their drinks and looking out over well trimmed grass.

Pedro was chairman of the 'Friends of Cuba' Association and they talked about that for a while. Then, as a seeming afterthought, Petersen brought the conversation round to the death of Bruno Pérez.

"That was a nasty business," he said.

Pedro nodded.

"Any idea as to motive?"

Pedro shook his head but Petersen thought he detected a hesitation. *What's that about,* he wondered. *Change the subject for a while, old interviewer trick.* "Play much golf?"

The powerfully built Cuban smiled and nodded.

"Any good?"

"Club champion the last three years."

"Wow." Petersen paused. "Back to Bruno . . ."

"Yes?"

"Could money have been involved?"

"What makes you ask?"

"No reason. It's that or a woman, often."

Pedro shook his head, drained his glass, looked at his watch. Petersen suddenly felt he was less welcome and indeed the meeting ended soon afterwards.

20

Petersen called Jane Oliveira again.

"What, you again?" she said, but in a friendly tone of voice.

"Yeah, me. Listen, I went to see Pedro Macias. I think he's hiding something."

"So you're a detective now! Why do you think that?"

"I asked him if he had any theories about the killer's motive. He said no, but there was something about the way he said it that didn't seem right."

"Did he roll his eyes and twitch furtively?"

"Almost. Well not really, but I interview a lot of people which involves asking a lot of questions and listening to their answers. They are sometimes a bit casual with the truth, so I don't think it's just my imagination."

"So, what next?" Jane asked.

"Why don't you go and see him. It can't hurt."

She thought, *This is a bit wrong way round, a journalist telling a detective how to do her job,* but she supposed he was right, it couldn't hurt.

"I might just do that," she said.

"What about the other guy?" he asked.

"Other guy?"

"The Israeli with the gun."

"What about him?"

"I'd like to go see him too."

She sighed and gave him the number. In for a penny, in for a pound. And the truth was, she had an awful lot on her plate. Taylor, her sergeant, was adequate but he was not the most imaginative guy in the world. Someone with a few ideas and, apparently, time to spare, was not unwelcome.

"Thanks. Is your name really Jane, by the way?"

"No, it's Juanita."

"So why the change?"

She laughed. "My police colleagues said Juanita Oliveira was a bit of a mouthful. They thought Jane Oliveira was snappier, I guess it just stuck."

21

I was in my cabin, vacuuming the floor. It was something to do. I vacuum about once a year but only if it really needs it. They say people who do their own housecleaning live longer and I like to believe that.

I was also waiting for a journalist called Petersen who called me and said he wanted to come and talk about Bruno's killing. He said he was a columnist for the *Herald* which I don't read. Sounded a decent enough guy but I couldn't understand what his interest in the incident was. I guess he'd tell me.

He arrived, got out of his car. White, thirties, tall and thin with a shock of sandy hair, slightly worried expression. He was wearing a frayed polo shirt and khakis, not very smart. I couldn't help noticing the fingers of his right hand were nicotine stained. We all have some vices I guess.

"Welcome to the Conch Republic," I said.

"I shook the hand of the mango man at the border but he didn't stamp my passport," he said.

For the uninitiated: In 1982, the mayor of Key West, the USA's southernmost city, was disappointed by certain aspects of US government, notably heavy handed behaviour by the US Border Patrol who, to discourage illegal immigrants and drug smuggling, set up a roadblock that stopped traffic, seriously limited tourism, and infuriated thousands of local residents. He decided, tongue in cheek, to secede from the United States and declare independence as a micronation with Key West as its capital and the chain of islands stretching from Key West in the south to Skeeter's Last Chance Saloon, Florida City in the north being referred to as 'The Northern Territories.' The Republic then declared war on the United States but surrendered quickly and applied for one billion dollars in foreign aid, which was denied. The nation's motto is "We seceded where others failed."

"Welcome, anyway," I said. "Grab a seat. What brings you here?"

We sat on an old wooden bench on my deck. "Bruno Pérez's killing."

"What's your interest?"

He looked at me. "What's yours?"

"He was a good friend," I said bleakly.

He inclined his head. "Sorry. I read the piece in

the paper and, frankly, thought it might make a blackly humorous column. But when I looked into it and spoke to a colleague of yours, Pedro Macias, I started to wonder about the whys and wherefores. Who would do that, and why?"

"I wish I knew the answer to that," I said. "It's a mystery to me too. So you spoke to Pedro. Did you learn anything useful?"

Petersen shook his head. "Is he your friend too?"

When I nodded, he paused a while. Then he looked as if he made up his mind to just blunder ahead. "I think he knows something about the motive," he said.

"Like what?"

"I don't know. But I think money was involved."

I hadn't known this guy more than a few minutes, but he struck me as perceptive. "Why do you say that?" I asked.

"I checked Macias out. His family is well known, as you are aware. Active in Cuban émigré affairs. There are even stories about a secret militia."

I stared at him without saying anything.

He shrugged. "Okay, I guess you wouldn't want to comment. But I imagine his activities require funding and money is a frequent motive for murder."

"Are you calling Pedro a murderer?"

"No, of course not."

But in the silence that followed, I began to wonder myself.

Petersen lit a cigarette. "Jane Oliveira said you carried a gun."

"Sometimes."

"You were carrying when she met you."

"It was a crime scene. I didn't know what to expect."

"Jane thought it was odd."

"Jane? You know her?"

"A little."

This is an unusual fellow, I thought. Intelligent. Inquisitive.

I wondered if he was onto something. For the first time I began to ask myself how Pedro had really come to be on the scene.

"Tell you what I'll do," I said. "I'll go and talk to Pedro again myself."

"If you learn anything, will you let me know?"

"So you can pass it on to Lt. Jane Oliveira?"

"I suppose I would have to do that."

"I'll think about it," I said.

22

I t was noon in Southern California. In the seaside community of Hermosa Beach, Ron Halfshaft was changing a tyre on his yellow '69 Ford Mustang convertible when his mobile phone rang. He wiped his hands on a rag and rescued the phone from the back seat of the Mustang.

"Yeah?"

"It's Kon. What'ya doing?"

"Not much. About to stroll as far as the pier and grab a taco."

Ron waited. There was only one reason Kon Feaver would call – he needed help. The two men had collaborated on a series of cases in the last few years, all involving the wealthy Carlton Tisch and his posh but bankrupt British sidekick Oliver Steele. In each case, Halfshaft had supplied a small but vital link in the chain of pursuit that led to catching the bad guys. His assumption this time was correct.

"There's this guy in Cuba. We want to trace him," said Kon. He explained about Bruno's trading activities and how Gaspar Gordon possibly fit into them.

Ron listened quietly, then, "Did Bruno have a web site?"

Kon hesitated. "I guess so."

"Can you find its address?"

"I'll have a look."

"Let me know."

"Will do."

There was a pause before Halfshaft spoke. "I think . . . I think I might need to come to Miami for this."

"Really? Isn't it something you can handle from L.A?"

"Nah, better to talk face to face, it avoids confusion. I'll catch a plane tomorrow."

This didn't make sense to Kon. He knew Halfshaft was nothing if not logical. A thought struck Kon. He checked the basketball schedule for the Miami Heat that was pinned up on the kitchen wall. In two days the Heat were playing at home in soon-to-be-renamed American Airlines Stadium on Biscayne Bay against – sure enough – the Los Angeles Lakers.

.   .   .

THAT EVENING RON HALFSHAFT caught the redeye from L.A. to Miami. Arriving next morning he checked into the Mutiny in Coconut Grove, then called me.

"I'm here, sleep deprived, but never mind. What's that website?"

I had done some research and found a number of references to Bruno's website which was not particularly confidential, so I provided it.

"Thanks," said Ron. "I'm on it."

"I need a street address for Gordon, not just his email," I reminded him.

"I understand. Finding his email is easy, his physical address will be the hard part, in fact it may be impossible. It depends how well he camouflaged it when he established his email."

"Just give it your best shot," I said.

23

One of Ron Halfshaft's more useful assets is a hyperactive brain. It stands him in good stead when designing video games which is how he's been spending a lot of time lately. He was intrigued about Bruno's death although not as emotionally affected as me – he's quite a bit nearer the autistic end of the spectrum – and pretty much cross-examined me about the possible suspects, until he knew as much about each of them as I did myself.

He showed particular interest in Dr. Hannah Mann and her sidekick Rudi.

"Wouldn't mind taking a closer look at them," he commented.

"Did I make her sound so attractive?"

His pale face grimaced. "Not her, I'm thinking more of the setup at that office. Why don't you call and see if we can go round there."

I wasn't too keen on that. Hannah and I had enjoyed a better-than-warm relationship so far but I didn't want her to think I was trying to forge a more lasting relationship, because I wasn't. However, deferring to the young Californian I called her and put her on loudspeaker so that he could listen in. I suggested we go round to her office.

"Things may get a bit busy here," she said doubtfully. "Rudi's out for the day. But yeah, I guess it's okay."

Reacting to her tone I almost backed away from the idea but Halfshaft nodded frantically at me, as if to say 'Go ahead,' so I did.

"See you later," I said.

A few hours later we rode the Jeep up to the 36th floor.

I apologised. "I brought Ron along, he's visiting from California. We can sit him at Rudi's desk and he can amuse himself quietly."

"Sure, I'll read a book on my iPhone," he said. "You guys pretend I'm not here."

We went into her office and she shut the door. We sat on the sofa across from her desk.

"Well?" she said.

"Well," I said.

"Here we are," she said.

"Yep," I said. We both laughed.

"Is your friend all right out there?"

"Oh sure. He's probably reading a computer

manual. He designs video games."

"He won't be able to use Rudi's computer, it's password protected," she said.

"No problem," I said lightly. But I was thinking, *That's a shame, he was probably hoping to do some spying on my behalf.*

She was not wearing the yellow dress today. Instead she had on green scrubs of the kind surgeons wear in the operating theatre. I couldn't help thinking it was overdoing the doctor image a little – her speciality of whole-body medicine presumably didn't involve surgery – but the coarse-woven linen tunic clung nicely to her upper body.

"How's it going with your search for whoever killed Bruno," she asked.

"Slowly," I said.

"Is that why he's in town – to help you?" She nodded towards the door.

"Something like that."

She stretched, arms above her head. "When are we going to get together again?"

"We're together now," I said.

"You know what I mean."

"Soon. When Ron goes home you might like to come down to the cabin," I said. I tried to sound enthusiastic. It actually wasn't difficult.

"In the Keys?"

"Yeah. Coquina Key, pearl of the Conch Republic."

She seemed slightly dubious. Was she more of a city girl?

I said, "What's your greatest pleasure?"

"Don't you know?"

"Besides that."

She thought for a minute, wrinkling her nose. "A gourmet meal in a nice restaurant."

"And getting all dressed up?"

She nodded.

She had just described my least favourite way of pissing away money, but I nodded. "We can do that."

We chatted some more but after a few minutes I noticed she was fidgeting and glancing at the door. I wondered if she had processed my words about Ron and was nervous about what he might be getting up to.

She stood up. "Let's see how your pal is doing." I wanted to check her in order to give Ron a warning but she was too quick for me. She flung open the door.

I need not have worried. Ron was sitting in a chair by the window some distance from Rudi's desk, staring out at the ocean.

"Heck of a view." He grinned.

"Yes, we're very proud of it," said Hannah. She was conventionally polite, but I sensed she was disconcerted, maybe even disappointed.

"We'll be on our way," I said to Hannah. "I'll be in touch."

She managed a smile. "For sure."

In the Jeep, going down in the elevator, Halfshaft said, "She's good-looking."

"No question," I said. "That was a bit of a waste of time, though."

"Don't be so sure," said Ron.

"Why? You can't have had time to read anything on their computer?"

"No. But going forward is a different matter."

"What do you mean?"

He reached in his pocket and produced a black metal object shaped like a hockey puck but smaller, about the size of a quarter but thicker.

"I assumed his computer would be password protected, it's normal. But I was able to slip one of these little fellows onto the back of the housing, underneath the desk. They attach magnetically."

"What's it for? Is it a bug?"

"In a sense. It lets me eavesdrop on the machine's activity. From now on I can see on my laptop everything that happens on their machine. They no longer have any privacy."

"Even when he looks at bank accounts that have their own additional passwords?"

He shook his head. "Won't help him. When he gets past a password, I get past it too."

"What about emails?"

"Same thing. I can read them."

"Incoming as well as outgoing?"

"Of course."

"What if he finds that bug?"

He shrugged. "He probably won't. But if he finds it he finds it. You'll be no worse off than before."

I wasn't entirely sure about that, but it's how Ron works, he's rather a bull-in-a-china-shop. But he usually gets away with it. Usually.

The Jeep reached street level and we exited the building and headed north. A few blocks later, as we were approaching the basketball stadium, Ron put a hand on my arm. "Er . . !"

"Yes?"

"Looks like the Lakers are in town."

"Really? You surprise me."

"Yeah. Can we stop. I'd like to grab a ticket for tonight."

I pulled into the stadium carpark. "We did well today. Get two tickets."

24

An hour later, Oliver Steele called me.

He laughed when I told him Half-shaft was in town, and that his visit coincided with a Lakers game. He knows Ron as well as he knows me. But he interrupted me when I said we were both going to the game.

"I have a luxury suite at the stadium."

"Really?"

"Didn't you know?"

"I sure didn't," I said.

"I've been a Lakers fan for years, ever since I lived in L.A. in the days of Magic Johnson and Kareem Abdul Jabar."

"Good for you," I said drily. I watch a game now and then but I don't go crazy over the sport.

"You should return those seats to the box office. Be my guests in the suite instead," Steele said. "We can use the time to chat. The game's a sellout so you should have no problem getting your money back."

It was quite a business actually, but I succeeded, and next night Ron and I arrived at the stadium carrying passes that I printed on my computer, bearing a scannable QR code that enabled us to waltz through various security gates and ascend to the level where the suites are.

It was a new experience for me. Basketball stadiums are big echoing places with lots of noise and brilliant digital advertisements flashing and changing colour with dazzling speed. The concrete-floored outer ring is a mixture of concession stands, toilets and stairs to the auditorium. It smells of beer and hot dogs, despite the chilly air-conditioning and resonates to the din of many feet as all and sundry clatter excitedly in.

But the elite, of whom Oliver was apparently one, have a different experience. We were shown by an usher through a private entrance and into another world.

The suite was about sixteen feet across. The inner side was open to the arena, but the other side gave onto a private open-air deck. We could stroll out and enjoy a drink against a backdrop of Miami skyscrapers whose lighted windows were starting to glitter as it grew dark. Hot snacks were on offer from a row of silver chafing dishes. A white jacketed attendant was fussing with the dishes as we entered.

"Champagne?" Steele grinned and waved an open bottle. He had the decency to look sheepish. I passed, but Halfshaft accepted a glass.

Steele glanced at the steel Rolex on his tanned wrist. "The game starts in twenty minutes. Things will get noisy then, but we can take a moment now to talk about Bruno."

I felt slightly resentful at his posh British accent and dismissive manner. We may be friends but his lofty air of entitlement can be quite annoying.

"What have you got to contribute?" I asked.

He ignored me. "About your list of suspects," he said.

"What about it?"

"Are we considering everyone?"

"Well, Emma Watts, Hannah Mann and Rudi have all behaved oddly," I said. "So has Rothman. That's four possibles. Isn't that enough?"

"It's a start," he said. "What about the others?"

"They are unlikely," I said. But Halfshaft agreed with Steele. "What about Pedro Macias," he asked.

"That's absurd," I said.

I may have sounded annoyed, because Steele said, "Ron's just being objective, listing all the options."

"Pedro's a good man."

Halfshaft shook his head. "Yeah, but think about it. We're agreed this may be about Castro's *dinero*. Pedro is super anti-Castro. He's also not made of money and he has to finance whatever he does with those so-called freedom fighters. Don't you think he'd love to get his hands on that loot?"

"It's not a realistic scenario," I said. "And it's insulting to Pedro."

Steele said, "Why? I know you like the man, but . . ."

I interrupted. "He saved my life, him and what Ron sarcastically calls his freedom fighters."

Halfshaft shrugged. "He was present at the scene of the crime. I'm just saying."

"No need to squabble, gentlemen," said Steele. "We'll leave him on the list and see how things go. Who else is there? What about the Watts girls?"

"I'm looking into Emma."

"What about the other twin?"

"Courtney? Nothing known. I haven't met her."

"Maybe you should."

"I've been quite busy." I tried not to sound indignant. Steele seemed to be taking things over despite having done none of the legwork.

"Of course," he said soothingly. He's bigger than me and supposedly good with his fists, but I could have smacked him.

Down in the arena, things were warming up. The players trotted out onto the playing floor and were introduced by a booming announcer. Deafening cheers and a lot of high fives and spotlights. A squad of minimally clad cheerleaders, smiles fixed, jiggled and jerked to more applause. Finally, all extraneous personnel left the floor and the game got going in a crescendo of noise. Even in our exclusive suite, continued discussion was impossible.

The first half was hotly contested, the lead alternating to and fro. The home team wore white, following tradition, while the Lakers sported their trademark bright yellow strip.

The crowd was raucous, cheering and booing with gusto. Mostly good natured but loudly partisan, they seemed to reserve their strongest emotions for the bearded figure of LeBron James who, as even I knew, was one of the best players ever. LeBron had history here, having moved from Cleveland to Miami, helped Miami win two championships, and then – inexcusably to Heat fans – bolted back to Cleveland where he won another. He then went to Los Angeles where he won yet again. He didn't seem to mind the booing and muscled aside various Heat defenders to help give the Lakers a two point lead at half time.

There was a large television screen on the wall of the suite. In the relative quiet of the interval, Oliver Steele drew our attention to it.

"We have a special guest, courtesy of Zoom," he said. He touched a button and there, in living colour, appeared the image of someone we all knew. He was an older man, grey haired, thin faced and deeply tanned with a fringe of white beard. I recognised my billionaire friend and sometime boss Carlton Tisch, sitting on the terrace outside his deceptively simple clifftop villa on Tortola in the British Virgin Islands, 1,200 miles from Miami.

He wore a Yankees baseball cap and looked like a shirtless beachcomber. Behind him I could see the pitched-roof outline of his house, a traditional Caribbean dwelling but one that looked suspiciously clean and sturdy.

"Good evening, Carlton," said Oliver.

Carlton scowled. He appeared grumpy which was par for the course.

Oliver turned to us. "Kon, you asked me to look into Bruno's Cuban associate Gaspar Gordon. I talked to a lot of people, including Carlton. He did some nosing around. Want to tell us what you found, Carlton?"

Carlton said, "There's a bank involved. It's called Integrity Bank Holdings and it's incorporated on Tortola, a few miles from where I'm sitting. Despite its name, it has a reputation for accepting fishy deposits from high net worth politicians in countries with one party systems."

"Dictators, in other words," said Steele.

"If you insist."

"Is Gordon a customer of the bank?"

"Not directly. But indirectly, yes."

"Explain."

"I was about to." Carlton sounded more than a bit irritated. "A few years ago, a huge number of records were pirated, or hacked from a law firm in Panama called Mossack Fonseca. A lot of financial chicanery was associated with the companies that it set up. There was a huge stink and Mossack Fonseca eventually closed down."

"The so-called Panama Papers," said Steele. "I remember. A bunch of famous names were mentioned. Actors – Jackie Chan's name came up. And associates of political figures. The brother-in-law of Chinese leader Xi Jinping and Sir Mark Thatcher, son of the British prime minister."

Carlton nodded. "So was Gaspar Gordon. He registered a company called Interim Holdings and its address of record is the same address as the office of Integrity Bank in Road Town, the capital of Tortola."

"Does that prove Gordon was dealing with Fidel Castro?"

"By itself, no. But he may have been."

I cleared my throat. "Carlton, I'm no financial expert, but ..."

"You can say that again," he growled.

I ignored him. You have to be tough with Carlton or he walks all over you. "What motive would Gordon have to kill Bruno?"

He scowled. "That's for you to figure out. But I could speculate ..."

"Yes?"

"Suppose Gordon and Bruno disagree over a commercial matter. Bruno threatens to inform the Cuban authorities of Gordon's fiscal cheating.

Gordon would be seriously at risk, unlike Bruno who had the sense to leave Cuba."

The arena lights dimmed. Steele said, "Half time's over. Carlton, would you like us to move the camera so that you can watch the game?"

"Nothing would bore me more," said Carlton shortly. "Tune me out, right now."

Oliver pressed a button and the grizzled financier disappeared.

In the second half, Miami battled mightily but it was not enough to overcome LeBron and his yellow-shirted colleagues who put on a late surge and won by ten points. As we were leaving, Oliver and I rode the down escalator together. He said, "Leave Gordon to me. I'll fly to Cuba using my British passport. You check up on the other Watts twin."

"Courtney? If you insist. Tough work, but some-one's got to do it."

"Good of you."

"By the way, that luxury suite . . ." I said.

"What about it?"

"Must cost an arm and a leg."

"It does."

"I thought you were bankrupt?"

"I am. So?"

"So where did you scratch up the loot to pay for something like that?"

"It's not mine," he said lightly.

"Whose is it, then?"

"One guess. You met him tonight."

"Carlton?"

"Who else?"

I processed that. "If that's the case and he lets you use it, you're getting a benefit in kind. Do you report the income on your tax return?"

He smiled sweetly. "You're pretty sharp, Kon. Don't get so sharp you cut yourself."

He doesn't often let the tough core show through his smooth British exterior but talk of money has a way of bringing it out, as it did then.

25

F ifty years ago:
    "Fix me a *Mojito*."
    Fidel Castro gestured to his brother
Rafael.

The bronzed forty year old dictator was relaxing on *Cayo Piedra*, his private island. The two Cubans had spent the morning scuba diving and were reclining on the jetty in deckchairs. Fidel's yacht *Granma* was bobbing at anchor in the bay.

Since coming to power in 1959, Fidel had consolidated his political supremacy. Those who could be considered his rivals had all been displaced one way or another. Camilo Cienfuegos, head of the armed forces, disappeared in a mysterious plane accident. The Argentinian doctor Che Guevara was killed in Bolivia by government troops. Several other senior figures were accused of betraying the revolution, convicted and shot.

Rafael mixed rum, soda-water, ice and green vegetation to produce two *Mojitos*. His relationship with his older brother Fidel was delicate. Rafael was the youngest of the seven after Ramon, Fidel, Raúl, Manuel, Pedro and Martin. His courage was indisputable, given his performance in the military struggle against the forces of displaced leader Batista, but between Fidel and Rafael there was no question that Fidel was the alpha male.

They sipped their drinks.

Fidel said, "I've been thinking about money."

"Money?" Rafael queried. "Why would Cuba need more money?"

Fidel nodded. "I understand your surprise. We have a steady income from the Soviet Union, thanks to Comrade Brezhnev. Our government is unchallenged. We have many homes, loyal supporters, and control of the administration and the military. "

"So I repeat, who needs more money?" Rafael asked.

"We do."

"Again, why?"

Fidel smiled, a cold smile. "I don't know of anything specific. But it doesn't matter. You never know what might happen in life. We should start diverting some of those Soviet roubles."

"You mean, to an account in our name?"

"Not in our name. Use a nominee company, with a neutral name. It never hurts to obscure the situation a bit." He stroked his black beard thoughtfully.

As usual, Rafael ended up deferring to his brother. "Okay."

TEN YEARS LATER:

Fidel and Rafael were in Fidel's villa at his spacious ranch outside Havana. Fidel's beard was flecked with some grey now. Also present was Hugo Macias, head of the Ministry of Finance.

Fidel said, "So it looks like the days of the USSR are numbered."

Rafael: "Unfortunately. It will mean no more money from Moscow, and that will kill us financially."

Fidel shrugged. "But it's happening. Gorbachev is anti-Soviet at heart. It's something over which we have absolutely no control."

Hugo Macias: "For Cuba it will mean bank-ruptcy." The mild mannered financier was respect-ful, but he sounded concerned.

Fidel shook his head. "Not true. It may mean years of hardship but we shall survive."

Macias looked troubled. "The government will be okay but the man in the street may starve."

"We'll give them ration books." Fidel frowned at Macias. "Don't get soft on me." He turned to Rafael. "We should do something about our private accounts. Are they in pesos?"

"Yes."

"That's not good. We should do something about it. Do you know anyone who could set up an account outside Cuba, in hard currency?"

"I'll make enquiries."

Macias stood up. His face was pale with anger. "Excuse me, I must leave. I have another appointment."

"Is something troubling you?" Fidel asked sarcastically.

Macias shook his head and, frowning, left the room. Fidel and Rafael watched him go. Their eyes met.

"A pity," said Fidel. "He's a capable person. Still, there are plenty of smart guys around, we can replace him without difficulty."

"My thought too," said Rafael. They sat in silence for a minute.

Rafael said, "There's a man in Santiago who we sometimes use when we want to deal in hard currency."

"In dollars?"

Rafael nodded. "He's a bit of a twister. By rights, we should have thrown him in jail years ago, but the fact is, he's been useful to us."

"How so?"

"For instance, he put together a scheme last year where a Cuban straw company imported cocaine from Colombia and sold it on to a cartel in the United States, earning dollars which were paid into the Cuban Treasury – indirectly, of course."

"That's unacceptable," said Fidel. "Cuba forbids drug trafficking."

"You approved the scheme," said Rafael gently.

Fidel scowled. "Talk to the guy. What's his name?"

"Gaspar Gordon."

AT THAT TIME Gaspar Gordon lived on a small ranch near Santiago in the eastern part of Cuba. Rafael went to see him there.

He explained what he wanted. They had met before over the matter of the cocaine dealership and neither man wasted time with pleasantries.

"I can help you," said Gordon, "but I shall need time to set things up with intermediaries."

"Intermediaries? Who are you talking about? These matters should be shared with as few people as possible and preferably none at all."

"Don't worry," Gordon said soothingly. "Discretion is second nature to the people I deal with."

"I need a name," said Rafael stubbornly.

Gordon sighed. He regarded Rafael as financially unsophisticated but also ruthless and he was the President's brother, so must be deferred to. "I work with a British stockbroker on Antigua called Watts – Harry Watts."

"And who does he deal with?"

"It varies but usually with Integrity Bank Holdings on Tortola."

Rafael smiled. "I like the name."

Gordon nodded. "I think you'll like the service too."

RAFAEL REPORTED BACK to Fidel a week later. "Regarding our peso accounts:"

"Yes?"

"The balances have all been transferred to a dollar account at Integrity Bank Holdings."

"Where is that?"

"In Roadtown, the capital of Tortola."

"In what name?"

"The name on the account is 'Pangbourne Plastics.'"

"Why Pangbourne?"

"Why not? Harry Watts suggested the name. Apparently it's the town in England where he grew up. It's also about as far away from Cuba as you can get."

Fidel sniffed. "Pangbourne, Pangbourne." He rolled the name around his tongue.

"I'm told it's a nice place, green and rural," said Rafael.

"Did you get a good rate?"

"No, dreadful. Everyone wants dollars and very few people want Cuban pesos, I'm sorry to say. We lost about twenty percent of value on the transaction."

Fidel shrugged. "Too bad. But it was to be expected. On the whole you did well."

"Thank you."

"Any new funds from Moscow should be changed into dollars and credited to the new account, as long as they keep coming in."

"Of course."

"Which may not be for long, alas."

"Understood."

"What about the Hugo Macias situation?"

"I'm working on that," said Rafael.

Fidel nodded. "Keep me posted."

In his office in the National Bank of Cuba's building in Havana, Hugo Macias was reading a printout of certain bank transactions. His assistant had highlighted in yellow several transactions between a Cuban peso account and a dollar account at Integrity Bank on Tortola. He circled the transfers, amounting to almost a billion dollars, all made in the period following his last meeting with the Castros. After a few minutes thought, he scrunched the paper up and tossed it in the trash basket under his desk.

A short while later there were raised voices outside his office and the door flew open. Two armed men in the blue uniform of the *Guardia*

Civile entered and stood to attention opposite his desk.

"Hugo Macias?"

"Yes."

"Please come with us."

"May I ask why?" But he could tell with depressing certainty what was about to happen.

"You are under arrest."

"On what charge?"

"Betraying the Revolution."

THERE WAS A SHORT TRIAL. The result was never in doubt. He was sentenced to imprisonment for a period of ten years. He was pleasantly surprised, as the standard for betraying the glorious Revolution, a much-used charge, was twenty years. He could only conclude that the cordial nature of his previous dealings with Fidel and Rafael had disposed them somewhat in his favour. Or, more likely, that thanks to his mild-mannered demeanour, they regarded him with contempt rather than as a serious threat.

Within days he was transferred to one of the huge cylindrical prison towers on *Isla de Pinos,* dismal relics of the Batista era, where he would serve out his sentence.

26

R on, lacking my prejudice in favour of Pedro, called him and asked to meet. Afterwards he told me how it went.

"We met in Wolfie's Deli on Miami Beach."

I laughed. "Is that place still going?"

Ron nodded. "Yeah. Pedro recommended it himself. They do a great corned beef sandwich – bake their own rye bread."

"So what went down?"

"We chatted for a while. I asked him, 'Take me through the moments of your arriving at Bruno's apartment – what you saw and what you did.' He asked me why. I explained that repeating one's recollection could stimulate new thoughts and might yield a fresh avenue of enquiry. I don't know if he bought that – he looked at me a bit sideways – but he played along with the idea and I took notes."

"Then what?"

"Then it got interesting. I put away my notepad and pencil and tried to create a relaxed mood. We talked about food – for a Cuban he's a good deli guy. I asked about his family history and how he came to be living in Florida. He talked about his grandfather Hugo, who spent ten years in prison in Cuba and then, after being released, escaped to Miami. Did you know Pedro was born in Cuba and came here as a kid of four?"

"No, I did not."

"Here's what's really grabbed me. I asked why his grandad was imprisoned."

"Why was he?"

"He was Fidel's minister of Finance."

"So?"

"He did the job for several years. He became Fidel's right hand man where money was concerned. Fidel trusted him, as much as Fidel trusted anyone. Then there was a parting of the ways."

"Why?"

Ron leaned forward, eyes shining. "Hugo disapproved of the steps Fidel was taking to set up dollar accounts at Integrity Bank."

"And that is significant how?"

Ron stared at me with something akin to pity. I get that a lot from smart people, not being an intellectual myself, so I didn't take offense.

"It means that Pedro probably knows where Fidel's dollars are. Hugo would have told him."

"Maybe," I said.

"At the very least, we should keep Pedro on our list of suspects."

"I guess," I said.

I didn't like the idea but I seemed to be outnumbered.

27

"This is Kon Feaver speaking."

I was on the phone to Courtney Watts, twin sister of the nubile Emma. My objective was to make contact, go see her and find out how she fit into this crazy puzzle.

"How can I help you, Mr. Feaver?"

The accent was English like her sister's but chilly, as if I were trying to sell her something she didn't want. Maybe I was.

"I'm a friend of Bruno Pérez who was at a party you attended a few days ago. He was murdered the next day. Your sister may have mentioned me."

"I've never heard of you. I don't talk to my sister much, we have different... circles of friends."

"But you recall Bruno?"

"Barely. What exactly do you want?"

This wasn't starting out well. But I hung in

there and she finally agreed to meet me. I would have preferred to go to her house but she insisted she was very busy, and I settled for early lunch next day at the Biltmore Hotel. She had a 'shoot' there later, apparently. Was she a model? Nobody had told me that.

THE BILTMORE IS the elder statesman of Miami hotels. Built in 1926, its architecture was inspired by the medieval tower of the Seville cathedral. It boasts 275 large and ornate rooms, four restaurants, two bars and an 18 hole golf course. The swimming pool stretches forever – Johnny Weissmuller is said to have broken a world record there. Past guests include Judy Garland, the Duke and Duchess of Windsor and Al Capone.

I was ten minutes late. I screeched to a halt outside the front entrance and tossed the Jeep keys to a uniformed bellboy. There may have been self-parking somewhere but I couldn't see it – probably a bracing walk away. *There goes $20*, I thought, but never mind, Carlton was good for it.

I strolled across the deep carpeted lobby to the restaurant. No problem finding Courtney – a brunette duplicate of Emma Watts, she was sitting at a table by herself, nursing a gin and tonic with three large olives. Severe would be as good a word as any to describe her. White silk blouse, dark jacket and skirt, large spectacles with black rims. Her hair was black, not blonde, so which of the twins was dyed and which was not?

She looked up, then consulted her gold Lady Rolex. She didn't say, "You're late," so I didn't apologise.

"So tell me how I can help," she said, as soon as I sat down.

I was pleasantly surprised. But why? It was only what a normal person would ask. Then I realised most of the other suspects I had talked to had been anything but normal, a bunch of freaks some would say. Her question made me rethink my view of her.

"I'm trying to discover who killed my friend Bruno Pérez," I said.

"And that involves me how?"

"As he lay dying, he scrawled a crude design on the floor in his own blood. It was in a star shape, which leads me to believe the killer may be one of the people with him on Star Island the night before."

She raised an eyebrow. "Sounds iffy."

"Maybe," I conceded. "But there's another thing."

I explained, as briefly as I could, about the Castro money at Integrity Bank. I tried to simplify the story but it was soon apparent that she had no problem grasping the facts. It was clear that she had a pretty good business brain and was highly intelligent all around, for that matter.

"It wasn't me and it wasn't Emma," she said with the flicker of a smile.

"So you alibi each other?"

"Exactly."

"I'd love to believe you, but your relationship as twins does weaken the alibi a bit," I said. "Presumably, you can see that."

"Fair enough," she said. "But the thing is, we went shopping the morning after the party and I for one can produce a bunch of receipts from various stores at several points throughout the morning."

"Emma's an unusual girl," I said.

"You noticed that?"

"Yes, I did."

"She has no filters for her enthusiasm," she said.

'Movies'n Massage' flashed before my eyes. I thought the comment summed up Emma pretty well.

We talked for a while. Courtney was not a model, but the fashion editor for a TV series. They were planning to photograph various models against the Biltmore's ornate backdrop. After half an hour a director colleague appeared at our table. Courtney apologised and excused herself politely, smiling behind the glasses.

By the time we parted I was two thirds

convinced that neither twin was the culprit. She wished me good luck and we exchanged phone numbers. You get a feeling about people sometimes, at least I do and, much as I tried to remain objective, I think I believed her.

28

Meanwhile, Oliver Steele set out for Santiago.

It is not possible, with limited exceptions, for a U.S. citizen to get on a plane and fly to Cuba nowadays. But Oliver had two passports. He was a U.S. citizen and also a British citizen, the result of being born British and then emigrating to the United States. So by using his British passport, he was able to fly to Cuba from any intermediate airport that had flights.

He took the shortest route he could which was via Cancun in Mexico. There were daily flights from Miami to Cancun and daily flights from there to Havana, just over an hour away. So that is what he did, using his US passport for the trip to Cancun and then the British one from Cancun to Cuba.

He arrived at Havana's Playa Baracoa Airport just in time to catch an afternoon connecting flight on a French-built twin turbo-prop ATR 72 'Firefly,' vintage 1980, of CubanAir. The noisy flight to Santiago took two and a half hours.

Santiago's Antonio Maceo Airport was small and surprisingly friendly after the long lines and tedious bureaucracy at Havana Immigration. He strolled off the plane and hailed a taxi.

He was pleased to see it was a small off-white Hyundai, about ten years old by the look of it. He chose it rather than one of the picturesque painted and polished fifties Chevrolets, prettier but less reliable, because its driver claimed to speak English. They all said that, of course, but this one, a stocky white middle-aged Cuban with a flamboyant moustache, rattled off a couple of phrases in a Brooklyn accent and Oliver judged his claim was real.

"Where to, boss?"

"I want to be near the centre of town, somewhere I can sit at a café and make phone calls. Is that possible?"

"Sure. There are cafés in the Cathedral Square."

"How long will that take?"

"Fifteen minutes."

"Let's do it."

Kon had given Oliver a phone number for

Gaspar Gordon that he had found in Bruno's address book, but Oliver's efforts to call from Miami and tell Gordon he was coming had failed. Static, crackling and hangups were all he got. He had been assured, though, that his mobile would work in Cuba; he would soon find out.

He leaned forward and spoke to the driver. "Your English is good."

"It should be, I spent twenty years in New York."

"Yet here you are in Cuba. How come?"

"I was born here. My wife was too. It's home."

"You prefer it to the dynamic atmosphere of New York?"

"Sure do."

"What about money? Cuban incomes are very low."

He shrugged. "I saved money when I was in the States. Gave most of it to my kids, who are still over there."

"But you are poor now. How do you handle that?"

"I'm not poor."

"I heard people only earn thirty dollars a month."

"That's if they work for the government. For workers in tourism, like me, it's different. We get the tourists' money."

"Like my few bucks?"

He laughed. "It all adds up."

They arrived at the square. The twin-spired cathedral was clean and white, pointed in pink. It gave off an atmosphere of orderly calm that compared favourably with what he remembered of more cosmopolitan Havana. The driver stopped at a café with outdoor tables on the shady side of the square. "How's this?"

"Perfect." Oliver paid him.

"Will you be in town for long?" The man asked.

"Until tomorrow."

"Need a place to stay?"

"Sure." This was working out well. When they parted he had the driver's name, which was José ("Call me Joe") and phone number, which he put in his phone's address book. Then he ordered a strong black coffee and phoned Gordon.

"Buenos dias?" The voice was quiet but clear.

"Mr. Gordon, my name is Oliver Steele. I want to consult you on a financial matter."

"Where are you and how did you get my name?" The English was accented but correct.

"I'm an accountant from Miami but I'm here, at the Cathedral square. I'm also a good friend of an associate of yours, Bruno Pérez."

A pause. Then: "You'd better come round. Do you have the address?"

"I do."

"See you in five minutes."

And shortly they were face-to-face.

Gaspar Gordon was old and bald. His face was shrivelled like a prune and his wattled neck looked wasted and thin inside the loose collar of his shirt. Oliver realised he should not have been surprised. Both Gordon and Pedro Macias's grandfather Hugo were in their prime forty years ago, when they had helped Fidel with his finances. They were now in their eighties or even more. But the little eyes that fixed Oliver with a direct gaze were as bright as those of a much younger man.

The thin lips curled in a slight smile.

"So you've come all the way to Oriente to talk to an old man about things that happened long ago," he said.

"How do you know it was so long?" Oliver asked.

"Because I've been retired for many years."

"You're right. It's about some banking arrangements that you made for President Fidel Castro."

"Ah." He motioned Oliver to sit.

Oliver looked around him. The terraced house was in a quiet street. It had not been particularly impressive from the outside but inside it was clean and elegant. Good paintings hung on the walls and, if Oliver was not mistaken, several vases that contained fresh flowers were made of silver.

"Your house is charming," said Oliver.

"Thank you." Gordon smiled faintly. "You're

probably wondering how a poor Cuban can afford such nice things?"

"You're a good mind reader."

"Before I retired I was one of the Administration's favoured few. Now, thanks to my association over many years with what you might call the ruling family, I am fairly comfortable."

"Let me bring you up to date," said Oliver. He outlined the events of the last few days, starting with Bruno's death which Gordon had not heard about. The old man drew a sharp breath at the news, shaking his head sadly.

Oliver explained about the party on Star Island and Kon's determination to find out who killed the Cuban entrepreneur.

Gordon was quiet for several minutes before speaking. Then he said, "What do you need from me?"

"I'm not sure," said Oliver. "But it seems likely that Bruno's death was the consequence in some way of a search by a member or members of that Star Island group for the money that was in Fidel Castro's offshore account at the time of his death. Money that is presumably still there."

"Yes, I think it's there," said Gordon. He was silent again for several minutes, then looked thoughtfully at Oliver.

"Let me explain a few things about life in Cuba," he said.

"First, anything involving the ruling family is

highly sensitive. Sensitive as in, if I speak out of turn, I am liable to be thrown in prison for the rest of my life. Which frankly is not likely to be long. But I would like to spend my remaining years here, not in some filthy dungeon, living on slops."

"I do understand, believe me," said Oliver.

"So you see I have to be super discreet. The only reason I talk to you at all is in memory of Bruno. I helped him set up his import business and contributed some seed capital from an account I control – note that I do not say I own it – in the United States. He was young enough to be my grandson and I suppose I admired his entrepreneurial character."

"Fair enough," said Oliver.

"Good. Having said that, here's my take on the overall situation: When Fidel died, almost my first thought was for the money in his account in Integrity Bank."

"How much was there, by the way?"

"Almost a billion."

"Dollars?"

Gordon nodded.

"I thought it would be less," said Oliver.

Gordon shook his head. "Remember, it was set up to receive the Soviet support payments, or a large part of them, and that went on for quite a while – from the time he anticipated the breakup of the Soviet Union to the date the breakup occurred, almost three years."

"Fair enough."

"Anyway, it was to be expected that someone would try and get their hands on it. His brother Rafael, for one."

"What's Rafael like?"

"Tricky. The other brothers, including Raúl and the farming brother Ramon, never liked him. I think it amused Fidel to share financial matters with Rafa just to annoy the rest of the family. He had a devious nature and liked to play people off, one against the another. It kept them all guessing. It's one way he survived local intrigue and US-inspired plots for sixty years."

"Has Rafael taken any steps to garner the money?"

"No, but he soon may."

"What does it take to draw down on the account?"

"A password. Also either Fidel's signature or else – and this is essential now that Fidel himself is dead – a power of attorney in prescribed form."

"Does Rafael know the password?"

"Yes, he does."

Oliver stood up and paced the tiles of the small living room. A fan spun slowly overhead. "That means he could move in at any time and clean out the lot!"

"Yes, it does."

"Why hasn't he acted?"

"I don't know. He may not perceive any urgency.

There's no reason he would know about Stanley Rothman and company."

"Speaking of whom, you were going to tell me who has contacted you."

"Sorry, I got distracted. Yes well, it was Rothman, of course. He and I have crossed paths before in connection with his recent attempts to open a casino in Havana."

"Do you like him?"

"No. And I told him I had no knowledge of Fidel's money."

"Do you think he believed you?"

"Probably not. But I don't care. Anyway, as you may have guessed, I chose to help Bruno. Which, alas, will not happen now."

"By giving him the password and a power of attorney in the correct form?"

"Yes."

Oliver sat down and drew a long breath. "Was that in the package Emma retrieved from the cabin in Stiltsville?"

"Yes, it was."

"Why Stiltsville?"

Gordon laughed. "That's slightly melodramatic, I know. But I have contacts in Miami who were able to make it happen – you don't need to know who – and it was a way of transmitting key information to Bruno without using conventional, and traceable, channels."

"But Emma Watts, helped innocently by my

friend Kon, nipped in and intercepted the package."

Gordon nodded. "Which means…"

Oliver completed the thought. "Which means Emma is the likely killer."

"It sounds that way," said the old man sadly.

"She talked her way into Bruno's flat, shot and tortured him into giving away the details of the drop, then killed him. A few days later she talked Kon into flying her to Stiltsville where she intercepted the password and papers."

Gordon nodded. "The young lady is not as sweet and innocent as she seems."

"Well she's British," said Oliver. "Perfidious Albion and so on."

"I wouldn't know," said Gordon.

"I would," said Oliver.

They sat in silence for a few minutes, the old Cuban and the young Britisher, tacitly lamenting the untrustworthiness of women. Outside, the shadows were lengthening. Gordon glanced at a grandfather clock in the corner of the room.

"I usually take something to quench my thirst around now."

"A *Mojito*?" Oliver guessed.

Gordon shook his head. "What is this obsession foreigners have with the *Mojito*? No, but if you look in the cabinet over there" – he indicated the sideboard – "you will find some glasses and a bottle of excellent sipping rum."

Oliver obliged and they tasted their drinks.

"Too bad Bacardi had to leave Cuba," said Oliver.

Gordon nodded. "Yes. Bacardi was founded here in Santiago by the way."

"I didn't know."

"It was in 1865. Don Fecundo Bacardi was a Spaniard who moved here and started a distillery. He and his son Emilio were both great philanthropists – the museum and a charitable foundation in the city were financed by them."

Oliver looked at the label on the rum bottle.

"Caney. I've not heard of that brand."

"When Bacardi's Cuban assets were confiscated in 1960 they moved their headquarters to Bermuda. The company's history since then is complicated – it was already a worldwide group but it is even bigger now, with production in many countries. It produces Havana Club rum, but not in Havana. It also owns Dewars whisky, Grey Goose vodka and Bombay Sapphire gin among other brands. To make matters even more complicated, the Cuban government now produces its own 'Havana Club' rum, so if you drink Havana Club overseas you may not know which version it is, the Cuban or the international."

"Complex," said Oliver.

"Meanwhile, the former Bacardi distillery here in Santiago produces rum under the Caney label.

So, even though it was not brewed by Bacardi, you are drinking, in my opinion, the real thing."

Oliver took another sip and swallowed appreciatively. "Before I get drunk, can we summarise the Bruno situation? What you've told me suggests that Emma Watts killed him, and that she is well placed now to raid the Castro millions. But what about Stanley Rothman? Although you did nothing to help him, he worries me."

"Why?"

"He's a dangerous man."

"He's certainly capable of following up by means of Harry Watts, my late colleague on Antigua, or his family. Watts had the same information I did because he was a link in the chain back when we set up the account at Integrity Bank."

"And he could have passed the information on to, for example, his children?"

Gordon nodded.

"That brings us back to Emma," said Oliver.

"And the other twin, Courtney."

"Yes, I had forgotten her. Would Harry Watts have known the password?"

"Yes, he would. So would Hugo Macias, by the way."

"Who could have passed it on to his son Pedro."

Gordon smiled. "I'm not making things any simpler, am I."

"That's okay," said Oliver. "I'm an accountant.

We welcome complexity, it's how we earn our living." But privately he was thinking that there were still too many suspects in the mix.

He looked at his watch. It was getting late and he sensed Gordon might be tiring. He wanted to get as much from the old man as he could.

"Does the name Hannah Mann mean anything to you?"

"Who?"

"She is a doctor in Miami."

Gordon shook his head.

"Never mind." Oliver got up to leave. "Thanks, you've been really helpful. I know you went beyond what's safe for you, given the situation here. You can be assured that I shall be discreet in how I use the information. I shall never reveal my source under any circumstances."

Gordon inclined his head. "If you can bring Bruno's killer to account it will have been worth it."

Oliver left the old man sitting quietly in his dark living room.

Outside, he phoned the driver Joe. "Can you pick me up?"

"Sure."

Joe took him to a "*Casa particular*," the Cuban equivalent of a bed and breakfast where he was greeted courteously and shown to a spotless room. Later, on the rooftop terrace, he attacked a supper of lobster mayonnaise and salad, washed down with a can of *Bucanero* beer. He was surprised how tired he felt afterwards, then realised he had flown from Miami to Cancun to Havana to Santiago all in one day so it wasn't really surprising. He set his alarm, went to bed and slept soundly for eight hours.

He retraced his steps next morning and in late afternoon found himself back in Miami.

29

Oliver called me.

"I'm back from Santiago."

"That was quick," I said.

"I had a squash game to play this afternoon, so I had to speed things up a bit."

"What did you find out?"

"Can't tell you now, I've got to leave for the squash court."

This was surprising, and also annoying. I wondered about Oliver's priorities. Did he rate a squash game more important than a murder investigation?

"The court's not far from your place," he said. "Why don't you meet me there and we can talk afterwards."

It was fairly clear that I didn't have much choice in the matter, so I agreed to meet him in a few hours.

.   .   .

FOLLOWING OLIVER'S DIRECTIONS, I drove south from Coquina Key to a destination a few miles this side of Key West, and stopped at a private home whose address he had given me. I got out and walked round to the back.

There was a flat roofed structure about thirty feet square with a single door and no windows. I assumed this was the squash court. Oliver and another man, who he introduced as Mark, were standing outside. We shook hands.

"You're going to watch? How exciting for you," said Mark cheerfully and, I think, tongue-in-cheek.

"The viewing gallery is upstairs. This is the southernmost squash court in the United States by the way," said Oliver importantly.

I climbed the stairs to the gallery and looked down on the court. The two players appeared and, after knocking up for a few minutes, started to play a match.

I don't know much about squash but it was soon clear that Oliver was neither as skilled nor as fit as his opponent. Each point seemed to go on for a very long time. I've watched tennis on TV and some of the points there are pretty long, but these were even longer. I noticed that, while Oliver was bustling around the court striving to reach and return his opponent's shots and getting progressively more exhausted, Mark always seemed to be just where he needed to be each time. It seemed to me that, on several occasions, Mark could have won the point and chose not to do so, but what do I know?

Anyway, when it was over, Oliver collapsed on the grass outside the court, reduced to a mass of quivering flesh.

"Close match, eh?" he gasped.

"Really? I thought you lost three nil."

"But they were close games."

It hadn't looked that way to me, but I said nothing.

"Well he's a many times national champion," he muttered crossly.

It seemed time to change the subject. "Tell me about Santiago," I said.

Oliver summarized what Gaspar Gordon had told him.

"He was right about one thing," he said. "Our murder suspects are still too numerous. The list is the same as the people who potentially have access to the Castro account, or the Pangbourne Plastics account, to use its official name."

"And they are?"

"Pedro Macias via his grandfather; Emma Watts via her late father; Bruno – now deceased – via his friend Gaspar, and Stanley Rothman who could have stolen it from any of the other three."

"Doesn't help us much, then," I said.

"Maybe. But it's like a jigsaw puzzle. It will make it easier to put everything together in the end."

"I sure hope so," I said.

30

Emma phoned. "What're you up to, Kon?"

"Not much."

"I have two tickets for Jimmy Buffett at the Olympia tonight."

I still wasn't sure what I thought about Emma, but an invitation to a Buffett concert was a no-brainer. "What time?"

"Starts at seven. Meet you outside at 6:30?"

"Okay."

Most rock concerts start late, but Jimmy tends to be on time. I've been to a couple of his shows, He sings many of the same songs each time but that's okay. If you're a Parrothead, i.e. a fan, you want to hear them anyway. If you're not familiar with Jimmy Buffett, his music has been described as 'Tropical Rock.' He wrote such highbrow favourites as "*Cheeseburger in Paradise*" and "*Let's Get Drunk and Screw"*. I was pleasantly surprised that Emma would be a fan, but whatever.

The Olympia Theatre, built in 1925, is downtown on East Flagler. It doesn't look like much from the street, just an unassuming theatre front, vaguely Art Nouveau, saying 'Olympia' in big letters and then, underneath, 'Gusman Center for the Performing Arts.' The external box-office has green wrought iron finials and cheerful flourishes in brown and green.

Emma was standing there in tee shirt and casual pants – one doesn't dress up for Jimmy.

"Thanks for thinking of me," I said. "How did you know I liked Jimmy Buffett?"

"I didn't for sure, but it goes along with the plane and the home on Coquina Key."

She took my arm and we went in.

The Olympia's interior is a 1,700-seat riot of rococo moulding and plaster corkscrew pillars. Its over-the-top decor, commissioned by Paramount in 1924 and designed by architect John Eberson to evoke a Spanish garden, recalls Miami's glory days of the 1930s when vacationing northerners, including many New York Jews, came south for the winter, stayed in the Fountainbleau and other Miami Beach hotels and looked for entertainment in places that reminded them of their New York home. Besides movies it hosted everything from vaudeville to Elvis Presley but it fell on hard times in the 1950s. Thanks to philanthropist Maurice

Gusman, who bought the ailing venue in 1970 and commissioned Morris Lapidus to restore the interior, it got a new lease of life and survives to this day.

I bought a box of chocolates for Emma and we sank into plush velvet seats.

"Not quite Jimmy Buffett," I said indicating the retro decor.

"But he's performed here before," she said.

A few minutes later, Jimmy bounced onstage, guitar in hand, and bowed low.

"Hi, Miami."

Even though he has never had a No. 1 single, Jimmy Buffett is said to be one of the richest singers alive. He is in his sixties now, genial, grew up in Pascagoula, Miss. loves to sail, loves to fly, used to live on St. Barts. His group, the Coral Reefers, play a fun, laid back, get away to the Islands kind of music with him as lead singer and guitarist. His style has inspired intense loyalty and spawned everything from restaurant chains – Margaritaville, Cheeseburger in Paradise – to merchandise – I have a pair of Margaritaville deck shoes – and even retirement communities for the over-55s.

What marks his concerts is that he just really enjoys himself and the audience can't help being infected by his good humour. He has also written some truly great songs. He started tonight with "A Pirate Looks at Forty", threw in a few new ones, and sprinkled some old favourites such as "Volcano", "Fins" and "Boat Drinks."

Two hours later came the moment everyone had been waiting for.

"Please be upstanding for the national anthem of Margaritaville."

Good natured cheers even before he began to sing.

He approached the end, everyone singing along:

"Some people claim there's a woman to blame,

But I know, it's my own damn fault."

The applause was ear-damaging.

As we filed out, Emma took my arm. "Hold on, I want to enjoy the atmosphere in the empty auditorium."

We gazed around, admiring the architect's riotous imagination for a few minutes. By the time we emerged into the street, the rest of the audience had dispersed and we were alone.

"Where's your car?" I asked.

She shrugged. "I came by public transport. I figured I could get you to drive me home."

"No problem."

I had left the Jeep in a dark, unattended parking lot a hundred yards up the street and when we got there I handed her into the passenger seat and we set out.

I had only driven a few yards north on Biscayne

Boulevard when I realised there was something amiss.

We were being followed by the same black Hummer. I noticed it as we were approaching the turnoff to the Port of Miami, the place where the cruise ships dock. It's a bleak area surrounded by a baffling one-way system designed to funnel traffic down to the quays where the huge ships lie ready to accept their thousands of passengers and waft them off to Cozumel, Antigua, Jamaica and elsewhere in the Caribbean.

I was about to drive straight past the road leading to the Port entrance when another car, a Mercedes, overtook me and swerved across my front fender. The only way I could avoid hitting it was to take the right hand turning, so I found myself heading along Port Boulevard towards Dodge Island and the port.

That stretch of road is long and one-way, so I had no option but to keep on going. I assumed that when I got to the island I could make a U-turn and come back to civilisation, but it wasn't to be. The Hummer continued to follow me. I was now sandwiched between the Mercedes in front and the Hummer behind. My heart sank as I realised we had been effectively corralled.

We proceeded along the narrow road.

"What's happening?" asked Emma. She sounded nervous.

"I don't know, but it's not good. I think we just got hijacked."

"Can you shake them off?"

"Not really." I kept driving, having no choice, and in moments we were on Dodge Island.

Dodge Island is basically a huge strip of concrete, big enough for major cruise ships the length of two football fields to berth alongside. There is a multi-storey parking structure at one end but apart from that the only structures are the long, open-sided roofed areas where passengers congregate with their bags while waiting to be processed and fed onto the liner of their choice. During the day there is usually a vessel loading or unloading. At this hour of the night there was indeed a ship there, but it was dark and the quay was deserted. The Mercedes, as I feared, braked to a stop and, having no option, I stopped too. The Hummer nuzzled up to my rear fender so that the Jeep was effectively trapped.

Out of the Mercedes stepped a suited figure and my fears were confirmed when I recognised one of the goons I had tipped into the water on the terrace of the Rusty Scupper. Not good. It was the short, heavily built guy. Unsurprisingly, he was armed.

"Nice evening," I said. "We seem destined to meet."

He waved his gun arm at me. "Raise your hands, wise-guy." He did not sound friendly.

I can move pretty fast when I have to and I reckoned I had to. Before he had a chance to take proper aim I stepped quickly forward, drew back my fist and punched him hard in the midriff. He doubled over, dropping the gun.

I bent down and scooped up the firearm. Then I backed away until there was a good ten feet between me and the sprawling man, who was winded but still conscious. I had a momentary feeling of victory.

I turned to face the group of cars, now twenty yards away. There was no moon so the night was dark, but streetlights at intervals provided enough light to make it possible to see what was going on.

My sense of triumph turned to apprehension as I registered the outlines of two people. One was Emma. The other was the other goon from the Rusty Scupper, the tall one. He too was armed. He had his left hand wrapped firmly around Emma's waist. The other arm, his gun arm, held a pistol to her head. I could have shot him, but even being the reasonable shot that I am, it was clearly not an option. For one thing, he was about eighty percent protected by the human shield that was Emma's body. For another, he only needed a light squeeze of the trigger to send the young woman to eternity with a bullet in the head. It was a standoff.

Fat Guy was getting to his feet. I trained my gun on him. He saw that and kept his distance.

"We seem to have a stalemate," I said, trying to sound calm.

"Yes, don't we," said Tall Guy, equally pleasant.

"What now?" I asked.

"Do you play chess?" asked Tall Guy.

"Occasionally," I said. "I know the moves."

"Then you know the difference between a pawn and a queen."

"Meaning?" I said. But I knew where he was going. Hypothetically, we could both fire, killing our targets. But while Emma was arguably a queen, Fat Guy was just a pawn in the game, if a rather bulky one. To put it crudely, his life was not of much value to either side, although it no doubt mattered greatly to him. I said nothing.

Tall Guy laughed. "I see you get my point. So here's a suggestion. You will put down your gun. I will not. You will come with me in the Mercedes to meet my boss. My colleague, who I think has almost recovered his breath, will follow us in the Hummer."

"What about her?" I indicated Emma.

"The young lady will get into the Jeep – I see the keys are in it – and drive herself home, or to your cabin, or to Ouagadougou for all I care."

I could not really argue with him, in fact I was starting to realise that he was no fool. I could respect the subtlety of his brain. I understood how his boss, whoever that was, would consider him a trusted lieutenant.

So we did it that way. Emma and I shared nods of understanding. Her face was as white as a bowl of grits but she climbed shakily into the Jeep and drove off, leaving me and the goons standing in the concrete roadway.

I was still apprehensive. I had trusted Tall Guy. If he had deceived me, this would be the moment to shoot me and toss my body into the flat, oily water next to the massive liner that lay at rest alongside the quay.

I sat next to Tall Guy as he drove the Mercedes back into town. He drove with one hand – competently, I have to say – the other keeping his gun trained on my mid-section.

"Been in this game long?" I asked conversationally.

"Off and on."

"Pay well, does it?"

"So so."

"I could make you a better offer," I suggested. I was reaching slightly, but it was just words after all.

He did not take the bait. He smiled. "I'm pretty well looked after."

We turned onto Brickell and I started to get a feeling that I knew where we were going. Sure enough, we turned into a tall new building I had been to before and the car elevator wafted us up thirty-six floors to the office of Dr. Hannah Mann.

31

It was nearly ten in the evening and most offices in the building were dark, but the surgery of Dr. Hannah Mann was ablaze with light. She and Rudi were both there. Fat Guy had peeled off in the Hummer, to who knows where? So with Tall Guy and me, there were four of us, I being outnumbered three to one.

Hannah and I exchanged glances. Her expression was hard to read. Not so much with Rudi, though.

He smiled broadly. "Hi, Sailor."

"Hi yourself," I said. "I underestimated you the last time we met."

Rudi's smile widened. "We all make mistakes. Yours may have been a whopper, though."

"How so?" I asked.

"You seem to have figured out what's at stake, generally speaking. But you may not realise how close we are to the end of the game. In less than a week, my friends and I will be richer by the thick end of a billion dollars."

I hadn't heard the amount mentioned before and I admit it shook me. A billion is a lot of clams.

He saw my surprise. "But you're getting too close for comfort, so I'm afraid you will have to be discouraged. Permanently."

That didn't sound good. I looked around. Tall Guy still had me covered, in spades. He moved to within six feet of me.

"I've been looking forward to this," he said. I guess he had a small resentment about my pushing him into the sea, down on Coquina. That had been a bit unkind of me. With hindsight a spot of subtlety might have worked better. Still, spilt milk.

His finger was literally caressing the trigger. I backed away and bumped into Rudi's desk. I'm not a praying man, never could figure out which religion was the best buy, but it seemed like time to make peace with the guy upstairs, whatever colour and shape he might be.

Rudi, thank goodness, had other ideas.

"Hold up. This is something we should run by Rothman."

Tall Guy backed away, his disappointment obvious. It was apparent that Rudi outranked him.

"Tie him up," said Rudi. "We'll leave him here tonight and take care of him for good in the morning."

Dr. Hannah found some duct tape – how could I have been so wrong about that woman? I was sat in Rudi's swivel chair behind his desk and tied up like the proverbial Thanksgiving turkey.

Tall Guy, Rudi and Hannah took their leave. Hannah even turned out the lights as she left. Thanks for nothing!

After they left, I took stock. Not an encouraging exercise. Enough indirect light came through the windows from the surrounding buildings that my eyes soon got used to the dimness. But there was little good about my situation. Rudi had moved the phone out of range and disconnected it, giving me a look as he did so that said 'forget it, chum.' I could have yelled at the top of my voice but there was nobody to hear.

It took me half an hour to think of anything helpful, and that not much. The screen on top of Rudi's desk was dark and the computer itself, in a metal housing under the desk, was inert. But a tiny light on the gunmetal grey case glowed green, and this made me wonder. I am no computer expert, the damn things baffle me and I try to keep well away from them. I can barely handle my mobile phone except to make phone calls, which in my view is what the devices should be confined to. But if I could coax the computer into life, perhaps I could send a message to the outside world via email or something similar.

My hands were duct-taped tightly across my

stomach. More duct tape round my thighs strapped me to Rudi's solid office chair. I was virtually immobile, as was certainly Rudi's intention. I wondered whether, by standing up and leaning forward, I could touch the keyboard with the fingers of my left hand.

I stood and leaned over the desktop. The heavy chair to which I was taped came with me, its weight stressing my legs and back. Craning forward, I could just touch the keyboard with my knuckles. The computer clicked and hummed quietly and the screen sprang to life.

Rudi had apparently been planning to write something. The screen displayed what looked like a document, although with nothing written on it.

I had no idea what to do next. There had to be a way to send email somehow but I had no clue how to find it on a strange computer or even, if I could, where to send it. The only email address I could remember was my own and there was nobody at home in my cabin on Coquina to read it, so that was no use.

I was depressed, I'm not ashamed to admit. So near and yet so far. I sank back, chair hitting the floor. After a while the computer went to sleep again and the screen died.

Half an hour passed. I reckoned by now it was close to midnight.

For want of anything better to do, I struggled

upright, lurched forward and thumbed the screen to life.

What had he been writing? Who knew? I tried to type my name by thumping with my bound fist on the keyboard. I found the K character on the keyboard and it showed on the screen. Then I aimed for the O, but got the I by mistake. Correcting it was well beyond my duct-taped ability. What about the N? Missed again, getting the nearby M instead. So the screen now read 'kim' in lower case. The pain in my back from supporting the heavy chair was getting intense, and I sat down.

After a few minutes I returned to the task. I hit the period key once but couldn't remove my fist soon enough so I got seven periods instead of one. Rats.

One more word, but what to say? 'Help,' perhaps? I tried but it came out as 'hell' which just about summed up my attitude. So I was left with the enigmatic line 'kim.......hell.'

The pain in my back was acute and I fell back in the chair. At least there was relief from the stress.

At that point, worn out by my efforts, I fell asleep.

32

Oliver drove back to his house in the Grove. He had actually learned a lot in Santiago and was mulling over what to do next. The decision was made for him when, minutes after he got home, the door bell rang. It was Ron Halfshaft.

"Thought I'd pop round and see if you're here. So this is the famous Coconut Grove! Did you get my calls?"

"Which calls?"

"On your mobile."

"My mobile doesn't work in Cuba." Oliver checked his phone and sure enough, there was a stream of messages from Ron, asking him to reply.

"Sorry," he said. "What's up?"

"Remember the recording device I attached to Hannah Man's computer?"

"Sure. Did you pick up any useful stuff?" Steele

was only half interested. He was tired. He firmly believed that most so-called urgent matters could wait until after breakfast tomorrow. But Ron was excited.

"Rudi has been exchanging emails with Stanley Rothman."

Oliver snapped to attention.

"I didn't know they knew each other. Rudi wasn't at the Star Island party. Hannah was there, but not Rudi. What did the emails say?"

"A lot of stuff. Where's your laptop, we can have a look."

Oliver let Ron start his computer. The Californian seemed to know his way around it instinctively.

"Here," Ron said. "See, they've emailed to and fro several times. The first series of messages was about Integrity Bank."

Just then, the computer beeped. Ron pressed a key and the beeping stopped.

"What's that?" asked Oliver.

"He's using it right now," said Ron.

"That's weird," said Oliver. "Ten pm is a strange time to be in the office. What's he doing?"

"He's typing a letter, or a memo or something."

"What does it say?"

"He's written 'Kim.....hell'."

"What else?"

"That's all. Anyway, his emails were asking Rothman for the password for Castro's account.

Rothman was explaining about the need for a power of attorney."

Oliver interrupted. "That typing – "Kim.....hell."

"It's 'kim' with a small k."

"Whatever. Is he telling someone called Kim to go to hell?"

Ron shrugged. "Search me."

Oliver looked over Ron's shoulder at the laptop's keyboard. "Does anything strike you?"

"Such as?"

"Well if someone was a poor typist and kept hitting the wrong keys, how else could that read?"

"Search me."

"Do you know anyone with a three letter name beginning with k?"

Ron thought for a moment. "Nope."

"Really?"

"Well – Kon Feaver, perhaps."

"Exactly. And o and n are close to i and m on the keyboard."

"So Rudi is typing 'Kon......hell?' Well I can understand he might dislike Kon for some reason."

"What keys are near l?"

Ron studied the keyboard again. "o? Kon...... heoo? That doesn't make sense."

"Try p."

Ron finally got it. "Kon......help."

"Exactly. I think Kon's in that office right now, and he's in trouble."

"Wow."

"Wow indeed!" Oliver retrieved his car keys. He also took the small bore Ruger automatic from the nightstand beside his bed, checked that it had a full clip, and shoved it in his pocket. "Let's go."

Ron hurried alongside Oliver and they jumped into Oliver's silver Infiniti. There was little traffic at that hour and in ten minutes they were approaching Hannah Mann's Brickell Avenue address.

The automobile elevator did not seem to be working at that hour, so they left the Infiniti in the street, and took the regular elevator to her office.

Kon heard someone at the door. He was able to wheel his chair across. A voice outside shouted "Kon" and he heaved a sigh of relief but he was not able to open the door. "I can't open it," he yelled.

"Get out of the way," shouted Oliver.

"I can't stand up," Kon gritted. "I'm duct taped to this bloody chair."

"Well move out of the way, any way you can. I'm going to put a bullet in the lock."

Oliver fired once. It did the trick and he pushed the door open. Kon sat there, still fastened to the chair with so much tape he looked like an Egyptian mummy.

"I guess that explains your lousy typing," said Oliver, getting to work with scissors. When he was done and Kon was rubbing circulation back into his wrists and arms he said, "You'd better stay at my place tonight. You look like you need a shower, by the way."

Kon nodded. "There's the matter of my Jeep which is probably sitting outside Emma Watts' place in Cocoplum."

"Emma Watts?"

"It's a long story."

"Presumably it can stay there until tomorrow."

WHEN THE THREE of them were back at Oliver's house, Oliver said, "Let's review."

"Okay."

"We have two objectives – finding Bruno's murderer and dealing with Castro's money."

"Dealing with?" Kon raised an eyebrow. "Nice phrase."

Oliver nodded. "The vagueness is deliberate. May I continue?"

Kon spread his hands.

"The two are related, of course. We have several suspects for the first, and they are all involved with the second, too."

Kon said, "Emma Watts, Rudi, Stanley Rothman or his surrogates."

"It looks as though Rudi and Rothman are working together, while Emma Watts is ploughing her own furrow," said Oliver. "But to my mind, finding Bruno's killer is much more important than the business with Integrity Bank.

It's a lot of dough, but at the end of the day it's only money."

Murmurs of agreement all round.

"So what do we do to smoke out Bruno's killer?" Ron asked.

Oliver said, "I have this strong feeling that if we keep an eye on whoever nicks the money from Integrity Bank, the killer will become clear – as a by-product, so to speak."

Kon said, "Emma seems to be the lead suspect. She has the password and the power of attorney. As far as we know, none of the others have them. What's to stop her going straight to the bank and cleaning out the account?"

"I think it's more likely she would draw out modest amounts, at least initially. Less likely to attract attention."

Oliver turned to Kon. "Kon, I think you should work on getting closer to your friend Miss Watts. You can start in the morning by going to fetch your Jeep."

33

I paid off my taxi and knocked on the door of the Cocoplum mansion.

The twin who opened it gave me a smile. "Hi, Kon."

But it was not Emma, it was the other twin, Courtney. Smart, bespectacled, sleek dark hair, the smile ironic.

I was actually quite relieved, as I was still not sure what I was supposed to say to Emma.

"Came to pick up the Jeep, did you?"

"Yep. There was some excitement last night, maybe Emma told you. Is she in?"

"She just left. I didn't get to speak to her except to say hi."

"Really, where's she headed?"

"Tortola."

Tortola, the home of Integrity Bank. That was not good news.

.   .   .

I DROVE the jeep back to Oliver's place.

"She's going to Tortola," I said. "We all know why."

34

Emma took her car, the Jaguar. She planned to leave it in the short-stay carpark at the airport. She didn't expect to be away more than a couple of days at the most. When she arrived in Tortola she would go straight to Integrity Bank's office in the capital, Roadtown, present her papers and withdraw ten thousand dollars.

The paperwork was in perfect order, but she realised she might be questioned about who she was and what the withdrawal was for. If asked, she planned to show polite surprise and say that she was just a member of the Castro family's administrative staff and that the ten grand was for cash expenses incurred in managing the Castros' overseas affairs. Something vague like that. The amount was deliberately not great. The worst that could happen was that they would say 'no.' Her thinking was to extract much more money over time; this first visit was just an icebreaker so that the bank's personnel would get used to her as an uncontroversial figure and raise no objection when she gradually increased her withdrawals.

She was nervous, no question about it, but it was a good plan and she would steel herself and follow it.

She reached the airport, parked the Jaguar, and got as far as the departure lobby before things started to go wrong.

35

Ted Petersen's suggestion that Pedro was deceiving me niggled. I tried to dismiss it from my mind, but I couldn't.

I knew where Pedro lived. I also knew where his *Águilas Negras* soldiers hung out in the Everglades, a place where he spent a lot of time.

I started by driving north to Hialeah and to his home on the golf course. I didn't tell him I was coming. That was for no special reason, I told myself, but I suppose in truth I was starting to view him in a new light, as someone who perhaps hadn't been frank with me, and who had reasons for that. It was a tough adjustment to make but I made it, because Bruno deserved my objectivity.

A maid answered the door.

"Is Mr. Macias in?"

"Mr. Hugo or Mr. Pedro?"

"Pedro."

"No, I'm afraid he's not home."

I guess I looked disappointed. She smiled apologetically. "I can see if Mr. Hugo is available if you like."

That could be interesting, I thought.

"Yes, please."

"May I know your name?"

"Kon Feaver."

"Wait here."

I did not resent the fact that she was obviously going to go and see if he wanted to talk to me. He was over ninety. Pedro had told me that he had suffered from several bouts with cancer although it was now supposedly under control. He seldom appeared in public.

She reappeared. "He'll be happy to say hello."

Then, in a confiding tone, "Not long, okay? He's not very strong."

"I promise," I said. She nodded, satisfied. I think she thought I was Hispanic, my appearance gives that impression sometimes and I don't mind. If anything, it's helpful.

I was shown into the lounge. Hugo Macias sat by the window in his dressing gown. I had seen him in public several years ago but never met him personally. He looked thinner and more frail than I remembered, his body shrunken and his face pale. He did not get up, but put out an arm and shook my hand.

"It's an honour to meet you," I said. I really

meant it. This was a man who had served his native country at the highest level, then been imprisoned for ten years in dreadful conditions, then escaped from Cuba to Florida where he was widely respected. A lifetime of service with no negative features was something to be admired.

He smiled. "I heard about your imprisonment in Cuba, that's something we have in common."

"Only a few days in my case."

"Still, you are lucky to be alive," he said.

"Thanks to Pedro and his guerrillas."

He grimaced. "One of very few good things they've done."

"You don't approve of them?"

"No, I don't. In my mind they are on a par with white supremacist outfits, or the fascist group that flourished in England under Oswald Mosely in the 1930s."

"That's pretty harsh."

"Perhaps. I tried to raise Pedro well. He is decent at heart. But military discipline, drilling with firearms, all that nonsense, he enjoys it too much. It's the first step down a slippery slope. He's out there in the Everglades today, he and Sanchez-Madera, who I thought better of."

So he was at odds with his son. Thinking about it, I was not surprised. The fact that Martin was there too, though, was unexpected.

When I left, I headed for the Everglades. Hugo Macias had told me what I needed to know.

The Everglades is a vast swampy area covering much of South Florida. It's largely uninhabited, overgrown with mangroves, home to alligators and, since their escape from a breeding facility damaged by Hurricane Andrew in 1992, Burmese pythons. It's not an environment friendly to humans but there are secluded areas of relatively dry land covered in thick jungle, one of which was the headquarters of Pedro's army.

From Miami I headed out along the Tamiami Trail, the long road that runs straight across the Everglades to Florida's west coast and then turns north to Tampa, hence the name.

About fifty miles from Miami I turned off along a narrow road that soon turned into a rutted unmetalled track leading through thick woods. It was bumpy and I was glad of the Jeep's four wheel drive. I finally came to a halt when the track ran out.

I got out of the Jeep and stood, wondering where to go next. There was nobody around. I had been here once before, when the *Águilas Negras* rescued me from the Cuban prison island and brought me back here by helicopter, but I was sick and close to unconscious at the time and my memory of how I got from there back to Miami was hazy.

It was incredibly hot and humid, the smell of rotten vegetation and damp mud pervasive and the only sound the humming of mosquitos. I swatted at the creatures but in moments there were bites on my neck and arms.

There was a rustling sound and a young man in khaki pants and tunic and black jungle boots was at my side.

"Hola!"

"Hi to you too," I said.

He looked at me, at first with hostility but then with growing recognition. "I remember you."

"You have the advantage of me," I said.

He nodded. "From last year. I was in the group that got you out of the cage in Cuba."

"I didn't recognise you. I'm afraid I wasn't at my best that day." There had been about ten guys in the group that had waged a fierce firefight on Cayo Piedra before bringing me back.

"I'm here to see Don Pedro," I said.

He led me through the tangle of vegetation, following a path that was invisible to me, and in ten minutes we emerged into a clearing.

At one end was what looked like an obstacle course. A dozen troopers were exercising on it, armed with rifles and carrying heavy backpacks, manoeuvring through the structures at top speed. At the final stage they threw themselves on the ground, took aim with the rifles and let off a volley of shots at prepared targets. Watching, and timing them with a stopwatch, was Pedro.

With him was Martin Sanchez-Madera,

wearing jacket and tie and looking somewhat ill at ease.

They greeted me with surprise. Pedro was the more welcoming.

"Kon, this is a nice surprise. Welcome to the future of Cuba!"

"This?" I asked.

"Sure."

"Tell me," I asked, "this training is impressive, but what exactly are they training *for*?"

Pedro laughed. "To be ready for anything, my friend. I've been explaining to Martin here, high on the list is the removal of the last Castro in government."

"You mean Raúl?"

"Exactly. As you know, there were many attempts on the life of Fidel, none of them successful. Next time, with Raúl, we shall succeed because we are a well-trained, highly motivated group, far superior to anything used in previous efforts."

Was he really talking about invading Cuba and killing the Communist Party secretary? Martin was listening and I caught his eye briefly. I thought he looked distinctly uncomfortable.

In a little while there was a break in the training exercises and I was able to take Pedro on one side.

"I had a visit from a journalist called Petersen," I said.

He nodded. "He came to see me too."

"He seemed to think you had shown a certain interest in some money that was somehow connected with Bruno's death."

Pedro frowned, an expression at odds with his normal genial manner.

"I never said anything to him about that," he said.

"It was more of an impression that he got."

Pedro said nothing. He fidgeted, brushing beads of sweat from his forehead. I waited.

Finally: "You may as well know," he said. "Yes, there is money, a lot actually."

Pedro described the situation with the Pangbourne Plastics account. I listened, but did not let on that I already knew some of what he was telling me.

"Where's the connection with Bruno's death?" I asked.

He spread his arms in a gesture of bafflement. "I don't know. Maybe nothing. But coming after the meeting on Star Island with those financially connected people, it's an odd coincidence."

I nodded and said nothing. The conversation lapsed and he walked away to talk to some of the troopers.

He had not behaved like someone involved in the murder of one of his close friends. At the same time, the questions in my mind, once they had crept in there, were refusing to go away.

36

I looked at my watch. It was late afternoon now and the shadows of the trees around the clearing were beginning to lengthen. The troops had finished their exercises and were putting their gear away in a storage cabin at one end of the clearing.

Martin Sanchez-Madera spoke to Pedro. "I really need to get back to the city, I have some work to do, to prepare for a lecture tomorrow."

Pedro paused in the middle of what looked like a motivational address to a cluster of troopers. "I have a few things to take care of. I'll be ready to leave in about an hour."

Martin looked at his watch, then turned to me. "If you're leaving shortly, can I ride back with you?"

"No problem," I said.

We made our way back to the Jeep and strapped ourselves in. I dialled the air conditioning up to maximum as we bumped along the track. Martin sighed. "That's a relief."

I laughed. "Not your kind of thing, this?"

"In more ways than one," he said with feeling.

I had been getting a growing sense that Martin wanted to unburden himself, and I was right.

"I have a real problem," he said.

"How so?"

"Pedro and I had come to an agreement about some funds that he could access."

"The Pangbourne Plastics money."

"You know about that?"

"He told me," I said.

"I agreed to make the withdrawal from the bank, which is on Tortola, using information that Pedro would give me. He did not wish to take that step himself."

"I know," I said. "And I think I know why."

"Hugo?"

"Exactly."

"I don't think I can go through with it," he said.

"What's the problem?"

He sighed. "Pedro and I have different approaches to the Cuban question, as you probably know. I favour a diplomatic solution whereby we isolate the present regime from the rest of the world but allow for a rapprochement later. It may take a few years but, given Raúl Castro's age, it will ensure that when the current president, Díaz-Canel, is up for re-election, that election is a real one – transparent, if you'll forgive the buzzword, and with a real opposition candidate. We need that for a free Democratic Cuba."

"Fair enough," I said. I don't follow politics. Every politician I've ever met has either been a liar, a cheat and a thief, or else at least two of the three. I may have been unlucky but I don't think so.

I paused. "Got anyone in mind as the opposition candidate?"

He laughed. "No prizes for the answer."

"You're a bit young."

"I shall be in my mid thirties by the time it happens. And I don't expect to win."

"You don't?"

"Not this time. Díaz-Canel is a smart guy, he'll be hard to beat. I've got my sights fixed on some time after that."

"That all sounds fine. What's the problem with Pedro?"

"Impatience. And a taste for violence."

"Really?"

"You saw those young men. They're fine now but they are like a younger version of Hitler's Brownshirts. He really does want to send a strike force to assassinate Raúl Castro. He'll do it, too, if he gets the financial backing."

"Hugo Macias agrees with you about the *Aguilas*. I spoke to him earlier today."

"That's interesting. Anyway, the bottom line is that I won't accept any of Pedro's money. I can't touch it. It would brand me as a militant which I'm not. And I won't help him by drawing it out of the bank."

"Has he given you the password and power of attorney?"

Martin shook his head. "I guess he still has them. If he tries to give them to me I shall refuse."

"Does he know that?"

"No. I'm trying to work myself up to tell him."

"So he has the papers with him?"

"He was going to give them to me today, so I suppose so."

37

On Star Island, Stanley Rothman was giving instructions to Tall Guy and Fat Guy. Actually, just to Tall Guy, since he was the brains of the pair.

"What I want you to do is drive to Hialeah and get next to this fellow Pedro Macias." He gave them Pedro's address.

"What do we do when we find him?" Tall Guy asked.

Rothman explained about the password and power of attorney. He repeated the key details until he was sure that Tall Guy understood.

"I need those papers," Rothman said. "Now get going."

THEY TOOK Fat Guy's Mercedes rather than Tall Guy's Hummer.

"Why are we going in this car?" Fat Guy grumbled, steering the saloon onto the freeway towards Hialeah. He was basically lazy and preferred to be driven rather than do the driving himself.

In the passenger seat, Tall Guy said, "Because Hummers are too conspicuous. Stop complaining."

They approached the Macias residence and drove past it, observing that the garage door was open. There was no car inside.

"He's not home. What do we do?" Fat Guy asked.

"We wait," said Tall Guy. "Pull over."

"Where?"

"Close to the house."

"What do we do when he shows?"

Tall Guy explained, and they settled down to wait.

Fat Guy had been looking puzzled all day. "What's so important about a bunch of papers?" he said mulishly.

"It's banking stuff, a lot of money is involved. Anyway it's not our business," said Tall Guy. "Just concentrate on doing your job."

A short while later, a car drew up outside Macias' house.

"It's him," snapped Tall Guy. "Quick, and remember what I said."

The two men, weapons drawn, leaped from the car and sprinted up to Pedro as he started to walk from the car to his front door. They converged on him, Tall Guy on the left and Fat Guy on the right, and pressed the barrels of their pistols into the soft part of his stomach from either side. Pedro was large and athletic, but he could feel the guns in his ribs and conceded as they manhandled him into the back seat of the Mercedes. Tall Guy climbed in after him.

Fat Guy coaxed the Mercedes out of its parking space and accelerated along the quiet street, round the corner and away.

Moments later there was no trace, outside the Macias residence, that the peace of the area had been disturbed.

"What's this about," asked Pedro angrily.

Tall Guy saw that Pedro was strong and vigorous and did not let the barrel of his gun waver an inch from his captive's stomach.

"I will shoot, you know," said Tall Guy. Their eyes met and it was enough to convince Pedro that his assailant meant what he said.

"What do you want?"

"You have some important banking papers. You know the ones I mean. We have to have them."

"Or what?"

"Or you will regret it."

But Pedro was recovering his self-possession.

"You have miscalculated, my friend. I do not have them on my person. And if you shoot me, you will never find out where they are."

Tall Guy nodded. What Pedro said was true.

However, he had been given specific instructions about what to do if this situation arose.

"Then we shall take you somewhere where you will have no access to them, so they will be of no use to you. That's the functional equivalent of your giving us the papers. So you lose either way." He smiled.

Pedro subsided in his seat. He racked his brain to find a counter argument. But he had to agree, grudgingly, that Tall Guy was right.

38

Emma joined the check-in line for her flight to San Juan and then Tortola. As she took her ticket and passport out of her handbag, she felt someone grip her arm.

It was Tall Guy.

"Good morning," he said politely. Her heart sank.

"What are you doing here?" She forced herself to speak calmly, showing only normal surprise.

Tall Guy smiled. "Oh, Mr. Rothman likes to keep an eye on his friends, make sure they are staying out of trouble."

"That's nice, but it's not necessary."

"Maybe. You going somewhere?"

"What if I am?"

He put out a hand, tweaked the ticket from her grasp, and looked at it. "Tortola, eh?"

"Yes. I thought I'd take a short vacation."

He nodded. "I'm not sure, but I think that's something Mr. Rothman would like to know about."

"Really, why?"

He laughed. "I don't know, it's above my pay grade, but he did mention Tortola specifically as a place he didn't want you to go."

She tried to pull away, in vain. Tall Guy gently but firmly guided her out of the check-in line and, almost before she realised it, they were in a quieter area of the lounge.

She began to understand at this point that Tall Guy's job wasn't only to prevent her from going to Tortola, he was going to take her captive. This was confirmed when he beckoned and Fat Guy appeared and placed himself on her other side. Before she could think, they hustled her into an empty corridor leading back to the car park.

Options flooded through her mind. She needed to cry for help, but she suspected they would make some kind of excuse and hustle her away. She had her mobile phone in her pocket but she knew that as soon as she started speaking they would snatch it away. Something ingenious was needed.

She straightened up and smiled at the two men.

"Okay, guys. I don't want to mess up my makeup, I'll come quietly."

"Sensible girl," smiled Tall Guy.

At any other time his patronising manner would have infuriated her, but she just nodded. As inconspicuously as she could, she slipped the phone out of her purse and tried to tap the 'camera' app. Could she do that without looking? Worth a try. As they walked she slipped it behind her back, aimed it at Tall Guy and pressed the button.

Picture taken. That was step one. She thought she could highlight the resulting picture and email it to her sister, but she did not do that immediately. Instead, she slipped the phone back in her purse. The moment would come.

She waited until they were in Fat Guy's Mercedes, in the parking lot. Tall Guy drove this time, with Emma in the back seat and Fat Guy beside her, on her left. That was when she eased the phone out again and, taking advantage of the low light and the distraction of guiding the Mercedes out of the parking structure, was able to silently forward the photo to her sister Courtney, all without a word spoken.

She didn't have a feeling of triumph, far from it. How Courtney would react to a photo of the back of Tall Guy's neck, she had no idea.

39

As it happened, Courtney was thinking about the whole situation just at that time. She did not really know what was going on – Emma had not confided in her – but she knew from her conversation with Kon at the Biltmore that something was going down that was potentially dangerous. When the photo came through, she stared at it, uncomprehending. She had no idea who the man was whose back and neck she was looking at, presumably a traveling companion. Also in the picture were Emma's own neck and shoulder.

She checked her watch. It was ten am. Emma could not have reached San Juan yet on her way to Tortola, so the photo must have been taken at Miami airport before she left. In the background was a sign saying 'SHORT TERM CARPARK' with an arrow.

It was a few seconds before she noticed something odd about the direction of the arrow. The people in the photo were walking *towards* the car-park, not away from it. That was surprising. Surely, if they were heading to the departure lounge, they should be walking away from the garage, not towards it.

Was that a bad sign? She knew enough about her sister's chaotic ways to wonder.

After a minute she called Kon on the number he had given her at the Biltmore. "Kon? It's Courtney Watts."

"What's up?"

"I just got a message from Emma and I'm not sure why. It's a photograph. It could even be a mistake, the wrong button pressed. But I don't want to do nothing. Can I send it to you?"

"Of course."

My phone pinged, telling me that the picture from Courtney was arriving.

"Let's see it, Kon," said Ron Half-shaft excitedly.

He and Oliver looked over my shoulder. It was clearly Tall Guy in the photograph, even though his back was turned.

"What the heck is Emma doing hanging out with him?" Ron asked.

Oliver said, "I know exactly what's happening. She's been intercepted and prevented from going to the bank."

"She would need the papers with her to withdraw money," I said.

Oliver nodded. "Which means Rothman has them now."

"And could raid the account at any time," said Ron.

There was a silence as we tried to think what to do next.

Then Ron said, "Let's see if Rudi's computer is alive, it might tell us something."

He fired up my laptop again and watched the screen.

"Look at this, something's going on."

As we watched, an email was being typed. It was eerie, seeing text appear silently on the screen and knowing that we were spying on someone in Hannah Mann's office six miles away, presumably Rudi.

The message was directed to Stanley Rothman. It was terse and to the point. "We had the Israeli but he got away. What now?"

"We should be able to read the reply if there is one," said Ron. Sure enough, a minute later, we saw, "Doesn't matter, he's not relevant. We have the woman here. We have the password and POA from her so we are all set."

Rudi typing again, "Then you don't need her anymore. Will you let her go?"

Rothman: "She knows too much. The guys will deal with her."

Rudi: "Like they did with Pérez?"

Rothman: "No comment."

Rudi's computer went quiet after that.

We looked at each other in dismay.

Oliver, who likes to act vague and amateurishly

British, was suddenly decisive. "It's time for an invasion."

"Meaning?"

"You read the emails. They are all on Star Island now: Rothman, Emma, Tall Guy, probably Fat Guy too. We have an opportunity. You read what they said about Bruno. We can believe Emma and Courtney's alibis now – it's clear that it was Tall Guy or his pal who shot him."

"So what do we do?" I asked. But I thought I knew.

"Ron and I will pay a visit to Star Island. Time to restore order."

"I'll gas up the Jeep."

Oliver shook his head. "You're not coming with us."

"Why not? Sounds like my kind of party."

"I have other plans for you."

He took me aside and we talked for several minutes.

By the time we were done and I left Kumquat Avenue, the plan was set.

Several hours went by, during which Oliver Steele made a number of preparations. Eventually, a big Cadillac Escalade SUV, rented for the purpose, drove across the causeway to Star Island carrying him and Ron. Both men were armed, with sidearms concealed under their clothing. It was late afternoon and starting to get dark.

They were stopped as usual at the island's gatehouse. For some reason shiny new Cadillacs tend to impress gatekeepers. Oliver said they were visiting Stanley Rothman – why lie when you don't have to – and they were admitted without question.

With Oliver at the wheel they drove smoothly to Rothman's house.

Oliver had considered breaking through the security barrier, but he did not like the idea. He hoped Rothman would admit him willingly. If it didn't turn out that way, busting in would be Plan B.

Plan B wasn't needed. Rothman was sufficiently self-confident or intrigued or both, that he allowed the vehicle through.

Oliver and Ron got out and waited in front of the expensive glass-panelled double doors. Neither of them had been to the house before. Oliver was impressed despite himself by the grandeur of the place; obviously no expense had been spared, either in its architecture or the decoration. He was determined not to show it, but Ron had no such inhibitions.

"Cool," he marveled. "Some pad." He fingered the white marble columns, studded with lapis lazuli inserts, that framed the entrance. "Looks like the freaking Taj Mahal."

The door swung open. Rothman himself had come to let them in. He stood staring at them.

Oliver stepped forward. "Evening, Mr. Rothman. This is my associate, Ron Halfshaft."

"Two of you? Well no matter, come in. And what's your function in life, Mr. Halfshaft?"

Ron moved from foot to foot. "Uh, I do stuff with computers, mostly."

Rothman's eyes narrowed. Oliver wondered if he was making a connection between computers and withdrawals from bank accounts. He cleared his throat.

"Let's cut to the chase. We believe you have Emma Watts here. Also that you have obtained the password and power of attorney necessary to withdraw funds from the Pangbourne Plastics account at Integrity Bank on Tortola."

Rothman smiled his unpleasant smile. "My, you seem to have been doing a lot of research. But you are mistaken about this plastics company, whatever it's called. I have absolutely no idea what you're talking about."

Oliver shook his head. "Nice try, Mr. Rothman. But last week I visited Gaspar Gordon in Santiago and we had a long chat about the creation of what, for convenience, we'll call the Castro Account. He explained how he had sent key documents to Bruno Pérez via a drop-off point in Stiltsville, documents you tried to intercept."

Ron was looking around. They were standing in a large, brightly lit entrance hall in which the white marble and lapis theme from outside was repeated. It led out to another large room and a terrace beyond – he could see the sea, darkening now, through full-length windows. To the left of the hallway, a broad staircase curved round, leading to the upper floor and no doubt a number of bedrooms.

"I suppose you're going to deny having Emma here also?" Ron blurted.

"Of course."

"In that case we know you're lying," said Ron

triumphantly. Oliver raised a hand to stop the Californian, he was talking far too much. But it was too
late, Ron had the bit between his teeth.

"See, I've been monitoring your emails on your
pal Rudi's computer."

Oh God, shut up, thought Oliver.

Rothman blinked. Ron's satisfaction at
confounding the casino magnate was far
outweighed by the damage done. Rothman would
certainly remember what he had discussed with
Rudi, including the killing of Bruno and the
planned permanent removal of Emma.

Rothman turned from Ron to Oliver and their
eyes met. Each knew exactly what the other was
thinking. The odds on any chance of resolving
their issues without force were slim to none and
Slim had just left Star Island to treat himself to a
nourishing dish of *Ropa Vieja* somewhere in Little
Havana.

"We can work this out," said Oliver, though
without much conviction.

"Yes we can," said Rothman. "But my way, not
yours." He turned back to the front door which
opened and in came Tall Guy, Fat Guy and Pedro
Macias. Unfortunately Pedro was at the receiving
end of the barrel of a gun held by Tall Guy.

Fat Guy was armed too. He trained his gun on
Oliver. Ron was only a couple of feet from Oliver
and they were each twenty feet from Fat Guy, so

they were both at extreme risk. Neither man had time to draw his gun, and Fat Guy was able to step forward, frisk them and remove their weapons.

Advantage Rothman.

42

I needed a boat. There was no time to fetch my own trusty vessel from Coquina Key, it would have taken the best part of a day, but I knew where I could find one.

A fishing pal of mine, Billy Spring, keeps a twenty foot launch at Dinner Key Marina, not a couple of miles from Oliver's house in the Grove. Big enough for my needs. I phoned him.

"Hi Billy, it's Kon."

"Hey Kon, how're they hanging?"

"Pretty good."

I told him about a quarter of the truth and arranged to rent his boat for the day. I mentally self-insured it against total loss, gunfire or Act of God, with Carlton on the hook for the premiums, and went to the marina to pick it up. It had a reliable diesel engine, reasonably quiet and was as easy to pilot as a golf cart, not that I would know.

The marina is barely a mile from Star Island and a short while later, after co-ordinating with Oliver time-wise, I was hovering a hundred yards offshore from Stanley Rothman's exquisitely vulgar glass and marble pad, right around the time that Oliver and Ron were scheduled to arrive there.

I killed the engine, floated silently and observed the goings on through binoculars. I saw Oliver and Ron greet Rothman and enter the hallway.

I could not hear what they were saying of course, but when Tall Guy and Fat Guy arrived, armed and with Pedro in tow, it was pretty obvious which way the wind was blowing, and it stunk pretty bad.

I gunned the motor and headed closer to the island. I stopped a couple of yards short, and not right opposite Rothman's place. I was close up against some other guy's house but nobody seemed to be at home there, which was just as well. Then I switched off and used a paddle to silently manoeuvre my boat close to Rothman's place. The house was about four feet higher than sea level, so mercifully I could not be seen from inside it. There was a rudimentary jetty, although I shouldn't think Rothman did much sailing, and I was able to loop my painter over a bollard and make it fast.

I sat in the bottom of the boat for a few seconds, breathing deeply and considering my next move. Not much to consider actually, events in the house could be moving fast and in the wrong direction. I needed to move along.

43

S tanley Rothman produced a gun of his own and aimed it at Oliver.

This is getting serious, thought Oliver. *I had better play for time.*

"Tell me," he said, "How did you even know about Castro's money?"

Rothman smiled. It was a knowing, annoying smile, lacking in warmth but brimming with smug self-congratulation. *He doesn't have to tell me*, Oliver thought, *but being the high-functioning psychopath that he is, having me and Ron at his mercy may loosen his tongue.*

He was right, because Rothman relaxed visibly, although he kept the gun aimed steadily at the middle of Oliver's stomach.

Bit by bit, he told the whole story, as Oliver had half expected he would. Before the portly little casino owner started to talk, Oliver unobtrusively switched his mobile phone to 'Record' in order to have a report of the conversation. He didn't know if he would be around for long to use it, but there was always a chance.

"I didn't know about the money, at least not at first," said Rothman. "But when Fidel died, in November 2016, I started wondering. What provision would *I* have made, if I was in his shoes? The idea that he would have stashed some funds overseas was a no-brainer."

"How did you know the funds were at Integrity Bank?"

"Again, I didn't, not for sure. But we financial folk are pretty savvy about that kind of thing, and I knew where to start looking. Hugo Macias was Fidel's finance minister during the period leading up to the collapse of the USSR and the end of Soviet payments to Cuba. I asked myself who he would have consulted, in order to set things up. The tax shelter universe may be world-wide, but in terms of knowledgeable experts it's fairly small. I've been around a while and I'm old enough to remember who the players were in those days. There was Milton Grundy in London, Zoltan Mihaly in Los Angeles and Jürgen Mossack's law firm in Panama. But the go-to name in Cuba was Gaspar Gordon, so I started with him."

"How did you get from him to Emma Watts?"

"It was easy. I got in touch with Gordon and told him I was interested in setting something up for myself, that I knew of his fine reputation but could not come to Cuba for obvious reasons. Who could he recommend?"

"You lied to him?"

Rothman stared, briefly taken aback, then waved a hand dismissively and continued, "He gave me the name of Harry Watts on Antigua, who is dead now of course, but from there I knew to contact his daughters, the Watts twins."

"What was the reason for the party you threw here?"

"Call me controlling, I just wanted to get all these fish in the same pond. I knew once they realised they were in competition for billions, something would pop, and it sure did."

"What about Bruno, what was his connection?"

"Are you kidding? Gordon's closest colleague here in the States? Of course he would try to use his relationship with Gordon to get hold of a power of attorney and withdraw the money."

"Why was a power of attorney necessary?"

He shrugged. "You don't just walk up to a bank and withdraw hundreds of millions. The paperwork has to be perfect. It would have Rafael Castro's signature – forged, of course but it would look impeccable. Gordon knew exactly how it had to be drafted and presented, so it was a matter of knowing to whom he would transmit this information."

"Is that the package that Emma Watts picked up from the Stiltsville cabin?"

Rothman nodded. "Yes. The package was meant for Bruno, of course. That's why I had Bruno killed. Then that little minx jumped in ahead of me. My people were in the cigarette boat, but she got ahead of them, thanks to your friend Kon."

Oliver frowned. "Kon actually had no idea what he was doing, he was just the chauffeur in the case."

Rothman shrugged. "Whatever! Emma had the password and other information already, she got it from her father before he died. But she needed the Stiltsville package to prevent anyone else from getting the same information. That's why she got your friend to fly her there."

Oliver said, "I still don't understand how she found out that Gordon had sent Bruno the package. How did she know it was going to be at Stiltsville?"

Rothman shook his head. "And I'm not going to tell you. If you can't figure it out it will have to remain a mystery."

Oliver was baffled, but he moved on. "What about Pedro? Why was he at the party?"

"I assumed he had knowledge of the Integrity Bank situation from his grandfather Hugo, but that he probably had no precise plan in that direction. He's somewhat unsophisticated." Rothman's lack of respect for the burly Cuban-American was obvious.

"And Martin Sanchez-Madera, why was he there?"

Rothman shrugged. "I included him in the party just to broaden it out and make it less obviously about Fidel Castro's money. The same was true of Rod Stirling, whose nose you inconsiderately broke."

"And Hannah?"

Rothman laughed. "My doctor? Cute, isn't she?"

"Just cute?"

"Well she's not stupid, but her assistant Rudi is the one with the real brains."

"You seem to have awarded Rudi an interest in the money."

"He works for me. He used to manage a gay bar I own in Las Vegas. I brought him here a couple of years ago when my last financial guy retired. I needed someone to handle money for me and Rudi does an excellent job. I make the decisions and he executes them. That way, my fingerprints are never on what happens."

"So does Hannah know about all this?"

"Not really. She knows Rudi works for me, but that's all. She doesn't ask questions. In return, I pay the overhead of her medical practice in that ridiculously expensive office."

"Including the automobile elevator?"

He grimaced. "A silly extravagance, but it amuses her."

"To recap," Oliver said, "Bruno liaised with Gaspar Gordon in Salvador. Gordon would send the password and power of attorney in a package to Stiltsville for Bruno to collect. But you arranged for your men in the cigarette boat to be there before him to pick it up."

"Correct."

"That sounds like a feasible plan. Sneaky but feasible. But then you went a step farther and had Bruno killed. Why?"

"It was a matter of timing. When we talked at the party, Bruno boasted he would go out and collect the package in the early evening – as soon as it got dark. A really bad idea, with all the people and traffic around. I explained that, but he wouldn't listen. He was pretty drunk."

"But killing him? Was that necessary?"

He shrugged. "My people went to his apartment to make him change his mind. They failed."

"How hard did they try?"

"They were authorized to offer him money to step aside. A couple of million. He wouldn't agree. I guess they ran out of patience."

"That's a tiny fraction of the Castro funds."

Rothman shrugged. "It would have been a fortune to him."

"So you killed him?"

Rothman looked at Oliver, surprised. "They did

that, not me. I'm not a murderer, Mr. Steele, I don't kill people. I don't lie either. That's what politicians do. I'm not a politician, I'm a businessman. I know more ways of not telling the truth than you could shake a stick at, but lying isn't one of them."

"Your hard men killed him, it's the same thing." Oliver indicated Tall Guy who was listening attentively, and Fat Guy who was frowning as if he didn't understand a word of what was going on.

Rothman looked at his watch and smiled. Oliver disliked his smile at the best of times but just now Rothman uncannily resembled a shark, and a hungry one at that.

"This conversation is enjoyable, but your presence is compromising my access to Fidel's money," he said gently. "You're a smart fellow and I can't have someone like you knowing what I'm doing with Integrity Bank."

He motioned to Tall Guy who moved forward.

44

Rothman raised his gun and trained it on Oliver's forehead.

Oliver smiled. "That won't get you anywhere," he said. He was glad he could muster a smile. It wasn't easy, because, inside, he had pretty much given up. He looked across at Tall Guy, whose finger was tightening on the trigger of his gun aimed at Ron.

Rothman shrugged. "I deem otherwise. You know too much, I'm afraid."

"I thought you did not kill people?"

He hesitated. "My word, you're quite right. Thank you for pointing that out."

He lowered his arm. "It will mean a bit more work for my colleagues here."

After that, things happened very fast. Two gunshots rang out, echoing off the marble floor and tiled walls of the conservatory.

Oliver shut his eyes at the crucial moment. But, not feeling any pain, he opened them again a moment later to see Kon standing in the doorway, thoughtfully blowing away the wisp of smoke coming from his gun. Tall Guy and Fat Guy lay on the floor, both dead.

"You took your time, didn't you?" was all Oliver could think to say.

Kon nodded. "Better late than never."

"This is worth a photo," said Oliver. He produced his mobile phone and took several photos of the two gunmen, both with their hands clutching weapons.

"That doesn't prove anything. You are going to be facing a charge of murder," said Rothman, looking at Kon.

"I doubt that," Oliver said, producing his mobile phone. "The audio quality on this isn't great but it's good enough. Anyone listening to a replay of the past ten minutes will understand that Kon fired only to defend me. They'll hear that you invited your men to shoot me. I think you're the one in trouble."

"Where's Emma?" asked Pedro.

In all the fuss, they had rather forgotten her. Pedro went upstairs and found her handcuffed to a radiator in one of the bedrooms. He brought her down.

"Well hi," Kon said. "You missed all the excitement. How are you doing?"

"My wrists hurt," she said crossly, rubbing them.

Nobody seemed sympathetic.

45

S omebody give me a hand cleaning up the garbage," I said.

Pedro knew what I meant. He stepped forward and we half carried, half dragged Tall Guy's body across the conservatory floor and out through the glass doors to the jetty outside. There we tipped him into Billy's boat.

"The other one too?" Pedro asked.

"Sure," I said. "And he's heavier."

Fat Guy was a lot heavier and we were puffing by the time we got him into the boat. There was a canvas tarpaulin in a locker under the seat and we wrapped the bodies in it, I didn't fancy having to explain to Billy Spring why there was blood on his nice clean boat.

"What will you do with them?" Pedro asked.

"Better you don't ask," I said.

Pedro went back into the house and I followed

him.

"We need some heavy weights."

There were a couple of white marble statues, one on each side of the front door. They probably weighed a hundred pounds each. I'm not really into sculpture so I couldn't guess their value but I'm sure they were worth a buck or two, and by the look in Rothman's beady eyes the bald financier was pretty unhappy as we tipped them off their stands and moved them, too, into the boat.

I found the last things I needed in the mansion's garage, in the shape of a length of steel chain and a bolt cutter. Pedro offered to help, but I chose to handle the last rites myself. It took a while and some ingenuity but finally, in pitch darkness, out in the deepest part of Biscayne Bay, the men who killed Bruno Pérez were consigned to oblivion.

I would have liked to have sent Stanley Rothman to join them, but it was not possible. But I had the satisfaction of knowing that, back at the mansion, Oliver had made a point of rounding up the paperwork Emma Watts and Stanley Rothman had been planning to submit to Integrity Bank to clean out the Pangbourne Plastics account, and burning them ceremoniously.

So for now the money was still there. I didn't know what would happen to it and frankly I didn't care.

But I did have a feeling of grim satisfaction at having personally disposed of Bruno's killers.

46

The end is nigh.

You thought it had come and gone? Well not quite.

A week later, I was getting ready to visit Carlton on Tortola for a social get-together with Oliver Steele, Ron Halfshaft and whoever else Carlton thought he would pull in – he has one of these parties a couple of times a year, just to keep in touch.

It's actually his wife Mimi who makes them happen. Carlton himself is gruff and unsociable to the point of being mildly psychopathic. Mimi is far more sensitive of the need to stay in touch and preserve the kind of amity that binds together the various skills of the group – Carlton's financial muscle, Oliver's accounting skills, Cathy Smith's tax knowhow, Ron's computing talent and my own, I'm not sure what you'd call it – relaxed stick-toitiveness perhaps – making it a force for good when needed.

Before setting out for Tortola, I decided that I would use my recently acquired knowledge to have a look at the Pangbourne Plastics account, just to check and because I could. So I logged onto the website, typed the password and account number and waited for a statement to appear.

Instead, up came a message saying 'Account Unknown.' The next screen informed me that the account was closed three days ago. In other words, the money was gone. All billion dollars of it.

Hello! Where did it go, you may hear me wondering?

It didn't really matter to me personally. I wasn't in line for any of it. But a billion is a billion. Not chopped liver. Not even a chicken salad sandwich on white toast. I resolved to raise the matter with the group when I got there.

It's ALWAYS fun getting to Carlton's place. Fun but arduous. The scheduled American Airlines flight to San Juan, followed by half an hour in a six seat boneshaker to Tortola's Terrance B. Lettsome airport, which is too small to accommodate regular jets. I drove a rented SUV over to the west end of the island on Tortola's crazily steep and winding roads and the last mile of crater-ridden dirt track to the villa.

Finally, the fabulous view as one steps onto his clifftop terrace, looking out across the bay to Jost Van Dyke island. A fresh breeze fans the brow – Tortola seldom varies more than a couple of points from a year-round eighty degrees Fahrenheit and there is none of Miami's sweaty humidity. I walked out onto the terrace, ready to sink into a deck chair, soft drink in hand and say hi to . . .

Say hi to Emma's twin sister, Courtney Watts.

No, I was not expecting that.

She, Mimi and Kathy Smith were cooling off in the pool. Mimi waved. I waved back. They got out and came and sat down. Courtney put on her black rimmed spectacles, stared and nodded at me. I had not seen her in a bikini before and it was a pleasant experience.

Small talk was all I could manage. Later in the day I was able to take her aside.

"I'm afraid your sister is upset with me," I said. Stanley Rothman was in jail in Miami on charges of murder (Bruno) and attempted murder (me) and Emma was sulking in Cocoplum, having lost out in her quest for a billion dollars.

Courtney shrugged. "Don't blame yourself. She lives on the edge. Something along those lines was bound to happen sooner or later."

"The money's gone," I said.

"Excuse me?"

"The Castro money. It's not there anymore."

"Oh, right," she said.

Carlton was passing and she beckoned him. "Kon is asking about the money," she said. She turned to me. "Do you know what a PAC is?"

"A Political Action Committee."

"Right. Well that's where the money is."

I stared at Carlton. "Is this your doing?"

The white-stubbled financier scratched his suntanned chest and shifted from foot to foot. "There's a Presidential election coming up in 2020."

"So?"

"So I shall put the money to good use," he said.

"But it belongs to the people of Cuba."

He shrugged. "Depends how you look at it. It was Soviet money before that. Anyway, finders keepers."

It had never occurred to me to wonder which side of the political fence Carlton sat on. "Which party do you support?" I asked.

"That's for me to know and you to find out," he said.

THE END

While it's still fresh in your mind, it would be really appreciated if you could write a brief review of *FEAVER PITCH* on the sales website where you bought the book. To go to the right place, press this link: PRESS

Then, why not read one of the following:

CASINO CARIBBEAN

Mild but dogged Oliver Steele is sent to Antigua to discourage a drug dealer turned internet casino owner who is terrorizing an elderly Florida bettor who has got in over his head. Twists and turns of murder and high finance in London and the Caribbean.

PRESS to order

CASINO EXCELSIOR

Oliver Steele has to step out of character to find the killer of a Las Vegas casino owner. Death stalks him in Los Angeles and in the maze of tunnels underneath Harrods. Intrigue on a yacht in Monte Carlo Harbour leads to a climax on the Caribbean tax-haven of St. Lydia.

PRESS to order

CASINO QADDAFI

Oliver is good at tracing missing millions but this time the funds are in Libya, a place of lethal anarchy after

Qaddafi's assassination. He has to outwit hostile bankers and the slain dictator's murderous henchmen.

PRESS to order

CASINO DE FRANCE

Oliver Steele is sent to Paris to track down a nuclear terrorist who is threatening the city. He wages a battle of wits with a ruthless lawyer and the depraved but wealthy scion of an oil-rich African republic who hates Parisians and everything they stand for.

PRESS to order

CASINO HAVANA

Oliver flies to Havana to save his friend Kon who has been imprisoned for smuggling refugees. He confronts a sadistic police chief and becomes involved in a pitched battle between Cuban soldiers and Floridian freedom fighters.

PRESS to order

JOBURG STEELE

South Africa is beset with political corruption and when Oliver flies to Johannesburg to trace fifty million dollars, the gang of criminal businessmen who blackmailed a government minister, murdered one investigator and kidnapped another is waiting.

PRESS to order

If you are reading the paperback, or if the links on your e-reader are not responsive, you can go to the author's website **www.grahamtempest.com** and order from there.

ABOUT THE AUTHOR

Graham Tempest is a British-American author living in Florida

COPYRIGHT

Made in the USA
Columbia, SC
07 March 2021